THE BACHELORS OF BROKEN HILL

Arthur W. Upfield

A Scribner Crime Classic

COLLIER BOOKS
MACMILLAN PUBLISHING COMPANY
NEW YORK

First Scribner Crime Classic/Collier Edition 1986
First Charles Scribner's Sons paperback edition
published 1984

MACMILLAN PUBLISHING COMPANY
866 THIRD AVENUE, NEW YORK, N.Y. 10022
COLLIER MACMILLAN CANADA INC.

7 9 11 13 15 17 19   20 18 16 14 12 10

ISBN 0-684-18246-7

Macmillan books are available at special discounts for bulk
purchases for sales promotions, premiums, fund-raising, or
educational use. For details, contact:

Special Sales Director
Macmillan Publishing Company
866 Third Avenue
New York, N.Y. 10022

PRINTED IN THE UNITED STATES OF AMERICA

CHAPTER ONE

The Place of Youth

Long, long ago the aborigines came and called it Wilya-Wilya-Yong. It was a dark, barren hill formed like a scimitar, its back broken, its slopes serrated and pitted and scarred, naked, sunburned, and wind-seared. One day a white man talked with a black man and learned that Wilya-Wilya-Yong meant the Place of Youth.

White men brought their sheep and a poor German named Charles Rasp was employed to herd them. Rasp gazed at the Place of Youth, climbed the slopes, and found what he found. He knew nothing of precious metals, and so travelled to the nearest city and purchased a copy of *The Prospector's Guide*. On his return he broke off a piece of the Place of Youth—it didn't matter where—and experts declared it to be loaded with silver-lead.

The fame of it sped across the surrounding sea-flat plains to the distant coasts of new-found Australia, and men came on horseback and on foot, in wagons and Buffalo Bill coaches, and they sank holes and rigged machinery. Others came and built a mining camp about the Place of Youth, which they called the Broken Hill. The camp became a shanty town named Broken Hill. Paupers became rich overnight, and rich men became

I

paupers in a matter of minutes. Champagne was a flood; water but a trickle.

Rasp and his partners faded out. Men were buried hastily in shallow graves: those who were lucky. Yet more men came to Broken Hill, lingered, departed—generations of them—and the shanty town became the third city in the state of New South Wales. Famous men came—engineers, scientists, industrialists; and eventually, in their turn, there came Jimmy the Screwsman and Napoleon Bonaparte, D.I., C.I.B., Queensland.

Broken Hill wasn't Jimmy's objective when he left Sydney on completion of a burglary, the planning of which had called for mental concentration over a period of three weeks, and Jimmy had looked forward with keen expectancy to a long holiday. He had arranged with a transport driver engaged in black-marketing to convey him to Melbourne—trains and aircraft being out owing to expected rigid police inspection at the state border. Then when the transport was nearing Albury and the driver stopped to converse with another of his gang bound in the opposite direction, he learned that, because of the escape of the Great Scarsby, all road transport between the capitals was being checked.

On the outskirts of Albury three utilities had met the transport, and into them went part of the cargo. With it went Jimmy the Screwsman, who eventually found himself at the inland town of Balranald.

In Balranald a newspaper informed Jimmy that the Great Scarsby was still at large, and police of three states were looking for him. He had been incarcerated during the Governor's pleasure in a criminal lunatic asylum, following trial for abduction in 1940, and as he had been a world-famed magician, hope of recapturing him was not high—in the view of the newspaper. Melbourne was now 'hot', even for Jimmy the Screwsman, and Jimmy decided to go west and take his vacation with a married sister in distant and far-away Broken Hill.

He arrived at Broken Hill on 2nd October, entering the city on the mail car from Wilcannia, and there, sick of big cities and tired by his mental activities. he proceeded to relax.

There is nothing parochial or bucolic about Broken Hill. There is no city in all Australia remotely like it excepting perhaps the golden city of Kalgoorlie. There is nothing of the snobocracy of Melbourne, or the dog-eat-dog taint of Sydney, in the community of Broken Hill, and there is no thoroughfare in Australia quite like Argent Street, Broken Hill's main shopping centre.

Argent Street is unique. Besides being a street of shops it is the universal place of rendezvous. 'Meet you down Argent Street' is the phrase employed by husband to wife, by friend to friend. You may pause before a building erected in mid-nineteenth century; proceed and gaze at a section of a mining camp of the 1870s; stay at a hotel the exact replica of those from which emerged the American Deadwood Dicks; eat at ultra cafés run by smart Greeks and Italians; hire a gleaming automobile and shop at lush emporiums.

Down Argent Street, Mr. Samuel Goldspink had begun business in the clothing trade when Queen Victoria found little at which to be amused. He had prospered less because of his own acumen than by the growth and the wealth of the city he had watched mature. He was an ingratiating little man, having an infectious chuckle

3

and a store of jokes against himself, so that his customers found it pleasant to be overcharged.

Mr. Goldspink was fifty-nine and a bachelor, seemingly hale and hearty, yet he collapsed and died inelegantly right in front of his own haberdashery counter. The doctor was dissatisfied with the manner of his passing, and the post-mortem revealed that the cause of death was cyanide poisoning; and, as it was quickly established that Goldspink had been in no mood to commit suicide, the effect was not dissimilar to that of a stick thrust into a bull ant's nest—Detective Sergeant Bill Crome being the chief bull ant.

Crome hadn't had a murder for three years, and to the unexpectedness of this one could be attributed his failure to net the poisoner.

On facts being winnowed from confusion they formed the vertebra of a common-enough background.

The time of the tragedy was three-twenty, or thereabouts, on a Friday afternoon, the busiest time of the week. The shop was crowded, and the eleven assistants were all hard at it, the most experienced serving two customers at the one time. Goldspink seldom served behind the counters. He was his own shop-walker, receiving his customers as his friends, talking volubly, escorting them to the departments they needed, and seeing to their comfort if they had to wait to be served.

From three o'clock every afternoon all the assistants in turn were given the opportunity to slip away to a rear fitting-room for a cup of tea and a sandwich served by Mr. Goldspink's housekeeper. Like the farmer who believes that a well-fed horse will work harder, Mr.

Goldspink believed in looking after his assistants, but in addition he had long proved himself a kindly man.

On her return to the shop, one or other of the assistants would carry a cup of tea and a biscuit to Mr. Goldspink, and sometimes he would invite a valued customer to join him.

Mr. Goldspink this Friday afternoon was chatting with a woman choosing handkerchiefs, and he told the girl to put the tea-cup on the counter as he was himself displaying handkerchiefs to the hesitant buyer, adding his persuasive powers to that of the girl actually serving.

The assistant said that the customer was seated at the counter and that her employer was standing beside the customer. She could not describe the customer save that she was elderly and a stranger. She remembered this because Mr. Goldspink put several artful questions to the customer in an effort to elicit her address. Eventually the customer chose her handkerchiefs, paid cash for the purchase, and departed without the receipted docket. Mr. Goldspink then had taken up the cup of lukewarm tea and drunk it. Whereupon he had turned half round to the main floor of his shop, staggered, arched his back, slumped, and collapsed.

Mrs. Robinov, the housekeeper, then had taken charge. She cleared the shop, locked the street doors, and called for the doctor who had been attending Mr. Goldspink for some time. The body was taken into the fitting-room and placed on the dressmakers' table. The doctor, being aware of the condition of Mr. Goldspink's heart, had not arrived until a full hour had passed.

The cup and saucer had been washed with the other utensils.

No cyanide was found in the shop or anywhere on the premises. As Mrs. Robinov was her late employer's sole beneficiary, she reopened business the day following the funeral.

The inquest was adjourned *sine die*.

The affair made Detective Sergeant Bill Crome most unhappy, owing to the fact that for the first time since being promoted to senior constable he had failed to produce results.

Old Goldspink had been cyanided on 28th October. On the afternoon of 10th November the wife of a mine manager reported the theft from her home of jewellery which she valued at sixty-five pounds. Senior Detective Abbot took charge of this case.

It appeared that the woman left her house on a shopping expedition down Argent Street, locking the front door and placing the key under the porch mat. On her return she retrieved the key, entered the house, and found 'slight' confusion. Thereupon she discovered the loss of the trinkets she was positive she had left in an unlocked draw of her dressing-table. A trifling case compared with murder, and yet perplexing because it was not stamped with the usual methods of any known local criminal. Abbot decided that the confusion was the result of a sudden decision to leave housework and go shopping, and that eventually the jewellery would be found by the owner, who had temporarily forgotten where she had put it. No one knows better than the experienced detective how frail is the human mind.

Frail! Crome's word for it was 'barmy'.

Early in December four hundred and seventeen pounds disappeared from the safe in the office of the

Diggers' Rest. There were no signs of the safe's having been tampered with. There were no unauthorised fingerprints on the safe. The key had never left the trousers pocket of the licensee, save when he went to bed, and it was then transferred to the pocket of his pyjamas. Drink! The licensee had been up to the hospital on the hill several times with delirium tremens.

Yes, Sergeant Crome was in no light mood as he strolled down Argent Street on the afternoon of 23rd December. The pavements were thronged with Christmas shoppers, and the street was alive with traffic flowing between the borders of parked cars, utilities, and horse buggies. Miners sagged against the veranda posts, weighted with parcels bestowed on them by their wives. Women gossiped in small parties, and their children tugged at their skirts in frantic demands for ices and toys.

Crome met and nodded to Luke Pavier, the Superintendent's son and reporter on the staff of the *Barrier Miner*. He met, and did not salute because he did not know him, Jimmy the Screwsman arrayed in tussore silk and a white panama hat.

From a jeweller's shop issued Dr. John Hoadly, who was large and young and damnably energetic.

"Day, Bill! Nothing to do?"

Sergeant Crome widened his mouth, pushed his felt hat to the back of his head, and then drew it forward to ride on an even keel.

"You'd be astonished at the work I get through while you squander your ill-gotten fees. How's the wife and the baby?"

"Fine, Bill, fine. Just bought her an opal pendant and

the kid a gold christening cup. Be up the pole this Christmas, with the wife in hospital, but it'll be worth it. The boy's a beaut."

"Naming him?"

"John. Wife insists."

The doctor's happiness lightened Crome's mood, and the sergeant smiled. "Nice work, Jack, but don't be a mug," he added seriously. "Make sure little John has a mate. An only child is a lost soul—I know. . . ."

A slight man wearing a white drill tunic and black trousers appeared, grasped the doctor by the arm, and regarded Sergeant Crome with black eyes tinted with indignation. He shouted:

"A customair! In my cafee! He stand, he bend back ovair one of my tables. He fall and breakit da table—smashoh. I go to him. I ask him 'What the hell?' He say nothing, nothing at all. He is dead."

"Your job, Doctor," Crome said.

Dr. Hoadly nodded. With the little Italian's hand still clutching his arm as though to be sure he would not run away, they entered the café, which was next to the jeweller's establishment.

The café was narrow and deep. People were standing with the startled irresoluteness of kangaroos warned of danger by one of their sentinels. Between the groups, like a ship steering between the islands of the Barrier Reef, the café proprietor led the doctor, Crome coming up astern.

An elderly man lay upon the wreckage of a table. The face was stained faintly blue. The dilated eyes tended to turn inward, and the bared teeth were irregular and tobacco-stained. Crome knew him—a retired miner living with his niece and her husband in South Broken Hill.

The customers were leaving the café, the sensation over and the prospect of being tabbed as witnesses enlarging. Crome was not particularly interested in them. Heat apoplexy. Many of these old chaps could not stand what in their youth they ignored. Old Alf Parsons was for it. Good way to go out—like a light.

The doctor made a superficial examination, and then crouched low and sniffed at the dead man's mouth. On rising to his feet, he dusted his trousers and wiped his hands with a handkerchief. He told the distracted Italian he would send for the ambulance, and Crome he drew aside and whispered:

"I'm not stating he died of cyanide, Bill, but I'm thinking he did."

Crome grabbed Favalora, the café proprietor.

"Where was he sitting?" he snarled.

There was cyanide in the dead man's tea-cup, which Crome presented to the analyst.

Crome kept on his feet for sixty hours. Asking questions, questions, questions. Statements, reports, theories, argument. Crome was semi-conscious when Inspector Stillman arrived from C.I.B., Sydney. Soft-spoken, sarcastic, bitingly insulting, Stillman caused Favalora to scream with rage, Mary Isaacs to weep, Mrs. Robinov to order him from the shop. Stillman caused Bill Crome to come within an ace of smashing a fist into his sadistic mouth, and Abbot actually formed his lips to give forth the raspberry.

A damn-fool woman complained that during her absence from home at North Broken Hill someone had

9

stolen one hundred and eighty pounds she had kept in the American clock on the sitting-room mantel. Barmy! Served her right. What the hell were banks for? Stillman, the swine! Ha! Ha! The wonderful Stillman was bogged down too. The mighty brain from Sydney wasn't able to produce any results.

Leads . . . blanks. Theories built . . . and pulled down. Questions, and ever more and more questions, leading nowhere, giving nothing. Stillman crawfishing out from under, pulling strings in Sydney to let him out and so leave the bag with Crome. Statements . . . reports . . . theories . . . conferences . . . disappointment . . . hope . . . disappointment . . . patience . . . patience.

The inquest on Alfred Parsons adjourned *sine die*.

CHAPTER TWO

Conference

It was a large room overlooking Argent Street, and only when the heavy door was open did the clacking of typewriters penetrate. Through the wide-open windows drifted the distant noise of mining machinery and the nearer sound of trams and cars. A room befitting the senior officer of the South-Western Police Division of New South Wales.

Superintendent Louis Pavier had never been known to betray irritability. He seldom smiled, and when he did the placid features blurred like a pond disturbed by a stone. There was a stillness about Pavier which had nothing to do with physical control.

One after another he was lifting reports from his 'in' basket, reading and initialling, and dropping them into the 'out' basket. It was routine work, the pulse of a virile community with his finger ever on the pulse, the patient mostly normal, and occasionally revealing bouts of fever. There remained three documents on his blotter when he pressed his desk bell.

The door opened to admit his secretary, who came to stand at his elbow and remove the contents of the 'out' basket. Pavier took up the documents from the blotter and turned slightly that he might look at the girl. She was young and good to look at.

"I must ask you to do these again, Miss Ball," he said, his voice placid as his face, and, like his face, betraying nothing. "You have a dictionary?"

"Yes, sir. I'm sorry, sir, if I've made mistakes."

"I have underlined them." He saw the mortification in her eyes. "You are doing quite well in Miss Lodding's place, and I don't expect to have from you Miss Lodding's efficiency. You will only gain that by experience —and perseverance. You are still attending night school?"

"Oh yes, sir."

"Stick to it. All right, Miss Ball."

"Excuse me, sir. The duty constable says there's a man waiting to see you. The name is Knapp. He won't state his business."

Superintendent Pavier glanced at his wrist watch, frowned, again looked up at his temporary secretary.

"Knapp!" he echoed, and then added: "Bring him in."

Coincidence. Must be coincidence. Plenty of people called Knapp. An entire nation once called a foreigner that name. A face he had seen at a police conference a few years back danced among the leaves of memory, and then the living face was beaming at him in his own office.

"Why, Inspector Bonaparte! How are you?"

"Well, Super. And you?"

"Quite a surprise. Sit down. Glad you called in on me."

The man dressed in an expertly pressed light grey suit sat on the indicated chair and crossed his legs. The amazingly blue eyes in the light brown face were friendly and happy, and from the inside pocket of the double-breasted coat came a long official envelope.

"In Sydney yesterday I lunched with your Chief," Bony said, toying with the envelope. "Among other matters we discussed was that of two poisoning cases which friend Stillman failed to finalise. I took it on myself to apply to my department for leave of absence to see what I can do about them, and I've been granted a fortnight. I have here a letter from your Chief. The matter is left entirely to you, as I made it plain that I had no wish to intrude into your domain save with your sanction."

Pavier accepted the proffered envelope, slit it open with a nail file, and extracted two letters. The topmost informed him that Inspector Bonaparte had been seconded to the New South Wales Police Department for fourteen days, and the other letter was a private epistle in which the writer explained that Queensland having loaned their 'precious' Bonaparte for fourteen days, would he, Pavier, see to it that Bonaparte was back with his own department at the expiration of that period, said Bonaparte being a notorious rebel. Dropping the communications to his desk, Superintendent Pavier said:

"Accept my assurance, Bonaparte, that we'll be very, very glad to have you with us. In view of the time that has passed since the last of the poisonings, two weeks will not enable you to accomplish a great deal, but we shall be very grateful to you for what you will, I am sure, do for us."

Bony completed the making of what looked something like a cigarette. The eyes were beaming, the teeth a white flash in a dark background.

"Actually, Super, I am expected to finalise the most stubborn homicide case in five minutes," Bony explained. "To have granted me fourteen days is excessively generous of my Chief Commissioner. He and I have been associated for many years, and I haven't noticed any mellowing going on in him. You've met him, of course. Forthright in his views—and his language. Tells me I'm not a policeman's bootlace, but I happen to be the only true detective he has. You see, Super, the cross I have to bear."

"Two weeks only," Pavier said firmly.

"Be not perturbed," Bony urged, lighting the awful cigarette. "I am a tortoise, and for twenty years my superiors have tried their hardest to turn me into a hare. Stupid, of course, because so many hares never finish the race. I always finish a race, always finalise the case I consent to take up."

"Consent to take up!"

"Precisely. Consent is the word. The number of sackings I have received no longer interest me. I have always been reinstated. Now don't you worry over me. My Chief knows my methods, my dear Watson. I have your co-operation?"

Pavier unknotted his eyebrows and slicked back his over-long white hair from the high and narrow forehead. The window light glistened in his dark eyes. They only indicated mood.

"Had I been unaware of your reputation, Bonaparte, I might have been angered by your—er—independence."

The smile on Bony's face evinced neither conceit nor arrogance, but assurance based on knowledge which is power.

"I am naturally impatient of red tape and regulations which are apt to bring on gastric trouble," he said. "So let us devote our attention to these cyanide cases which Stillman, as the living worshipper of the Civil Machine, so signally failed to finalise. I have never failed, due, I believe, to an iron determination not to be sidetracked by the whims of a superior, and to an inherent gift of perseverence. I am not a Stillman who can ignore defeat. I dare not fail, for failure would mean the murder of the one thing which keeps me from the camps of the aborigines. To explain further would occupy too much time. I hope to finalise these poisonings within the fortnight. If not, then, with or without official sanction, I shall continue my investigation until I do discover the poisoner."

"But you must obey orders," expostulated Pavier, whose whole career had been governed by obedience to orders and the issuing of orders. "One cannot be a useful member of any organisation and not obey the orders of the organisation."

"I obey an order when it suits me," Bony said, and Pavier marvelled that he could feel no ire. "I am unique because I stand midway between the white and black races, having all the virtues of the white race and very few vices of the black race. I have mastered the art of taking pains, and I was born with the gift of observation. I never hurry in my hunt for a murderer, but I never delay my approach. You can find me a corner? There will be much research work to do."

"Yes, we can give you an office."

"Thank you. H'm! One o'clock. Perhaps you would like to ask me to lunch."

"Your suggestion is acceptable," Pavier said dryly. "A moment."

He ordered Switch to put him through to the Sunset Club and spoke to the head steward, and when he rose from his desk he was undecided whether to laugh at himself or this extraordinary Bonaparte.

"Let's go," he said, and went for his hat.

He walked erect, the constable's training still evident. Taller than Bony, he moved like an imponderable sea wave. A man at whom other men looked more than once and to be with was to lose something of oneself. Having crossed the road, a young man bailed them up with the greeting:

"Hallo, there! Trailin' already?"

He was blue-eyed and fair-haired, and his nose and mouth made denial of him impossible. Pavier regarded him calmly enough, but there was resignation in his voice.

"My son Luke. Friend of mine, Luke."

"Cheers!" Luke Pavier nodded coolly to Bony. "Saw you leave the Sydney plane this morning, Mr. Friend. Name on passenger list Bona Knapp. Same name in the register at the Western Mail Hotel. Glad to know you, Mr. Friend."

"And I you, Mr. Pavier."

"I trust that Mrs. Napoleon Bonaparte is quite well?" asked the young man, and Pavier muttered:

"Damn! Now please don't publish Inspector Bonaparte's arrival."

"All right—for a price," argued the young man, who laughed at his father and winked at Bony.

"The price?" Bony murmured.

"A promise to let me in at the showdown. It's easy guessing why you're here."

"You might not be worth it. What d'you know of the people of Broken Hill?"

"Everything," Luke Pavier claimed. "I know everyone. I know all the two-up schools, all the baccarat joints, all the molls. I know the inside of every mine and the contents of every mining manager's report to his directors before they get it."

"But you don't know who poisoned two men with cyanide," interposed Bony. "Be patient, and some day I'll tell you. You will co-operate?"

"I always co-operate with the police."

"Rubbish," inserted his father.

The young man smiled, waved a hand, departed, and his father conducted Bony to the Sunset Club, where they were given a table in an alcove.

"I think you'll get along well with Crome," Pavier said when they were engaged with cheese and celery. "Crome is a good man, but we don't have the opportunities of unravelling subtle crime. He's the chief of the Detective Office. You'll come to understand all our limitations, and our difficulties in a place like Broken Hill. People here are prosperous, healthy, and clean mentally as well as physically. Contented, too, because of the amity between the workers and the companies— not without former years of strife. Before these cyaniding cases, crime hasn't been serious for several decades, and often the visiting magistrate was presented with the white gloves of a clean register."

"Your son Luke—is he a journalist?"

"He is, and, I'm told, a good one. With him his paper

comes first, as with me the department does. At home we never talk shop. He'll use you up if you're not wary, but he can be helpful. He flayed Stillman in his paper."

"I have always found Stillman a most unpleasant person," Bony said. "His observations are coloured by a singularly distorted outlook. It was hinted to me that a change in the commissionership might be to his detriment."

"I've always impressed on the minds of young constables that there isn't the slightest excuse for a policeman not being a gentleman," Pavier observed. "You obtained a copy of Stillman's official summary, of course?"

"Yes. Disappointing in real value. Throws much of the onus on Sergeant Crome for having permitted the customers to leave Favalora's Café before questioning. In fact, Stillman wriggled out by blaming all and sundry, excluding himself."

"No one blames Crome for that affair at the café more than Sergeant Crome," Pavier said. "The circumstances, however, relieve him of some of the blame. It was a hot and sultry day, unusual for Broken Hill, where the summers are very hot with little if any humidity. The temperature today, for instance, is somewhere about ninety-eight degrees but isn't trying. Old Parsons was just the type to collapse from the heat. And Crome knew him, too."

"Crome didn't get along with Stillman?"

The Superintendent gave one of his rare smiles, and this one was minus laughter. Bony side-stepped the subject.

"If Crome will work with me," he said, "we'll put

Stillman hard and fast into his box. Well, thanks for the lunch."

Pavier went first down the stairs to the street, satisfied that Bonaparte and Crome, and Crome's staff, would team well, and pleased that first impressions had not endured. Arrived on the pavement, he heard Bony exclaim:

"Jimmy! How are you, Jimmy?"

Pavier did not hear the ensuing conversation, crossing the street to Headquarters, and Bony kept an eye on the Superintendent, smiling at Jimmy the Screwsman, who was emphatically uncertain of the situation.

"On holidays, Inspector," asserted Jimmy, inwardly cursing his luck. He watched the smile fade from the blue eyes. "Honest, Inspector. Haven't taken a trick now for years—true."

"Of course you haven't, Jimmy. Been long in Broken Hill?"

"Since October. Decided to go straight, and found the only chance of doing that was to get right away from the cities."

"So you were here when Goldspink was murdered, and a man named Parsons, eh?"

"Now look here, Inspector," pleaded Jimmy. "You know I wouldn't go in for murder. You know very well I've never carried a gun or ever done any bashing."

"Working?"

"N-no. Holidaying, as I told you."

"I marvel that you were not picked up by the boys from Sydney—Inspector Stillman, too."

"Never showed out," declared Jimmy, wishing the pavement would become mud soft enough to bury him.

The terrifying blue eyes went on prodding his ego with blue-hot needles.

"Where living?" came the barked question.

"Twenty-two King Street, South Broken Hill."

"Much left of the cash you took from the bookmaker's flat in King's Cross?"

Jimmy fought a losing fight. The blue eyes were terrific.

"Most of it," he confessed. "I'll do a deal, Inspector. I'll return the lot if you——"

"Don't bargain with me, Jimmy. I'll issue orders. You will stay put. If you clear away from Broken Hill without my permission, I'll track you ten times round the world if necessary to get you put away for a nice seven years of the best." The blue eyes softened, and Jimmy was truly grateful. "Be around, and don't get yourself arrested. By the way, your tie is a monstrosity. Run along and buy yourself others at the shop owned by the late Sam Goldspink. Take afternoon tea at Favalora's Café and make love to the waitress who served old Parsons with his last cup of tea. Clear, Jimmy?"

"You want me to work with you, Inspector?"

"I didn't actually say so, Jimmy. Some distance along the street I see a young man who is a reporter. You don't know me at all well. We met, you will remember, at a reception at Government House in Brisbane."

Thoroughly shocked, Jimmy the Screwsman sauntered down Argent Street.

CHAPTER THREE

Problems for Bony

Bony was delighted with his office, a small room situated at the end of a corridor and plainly furnished. He had only to turn in his chair and thump the wall to summon Sergeant Crome.

He liked Crome at their first meeting. Big, inclined to stoutness, not much hair, and grey at that, Crome was both dynamic and kindly, impatient with himself and tolerant unto others, and very early Bony sensed that he was perturbed by the discovery that he had not been equal to events. What Crome needed was a renewal of confidence.

"Sit down, Crome, and smoke if you want to," Bony told him when Pavier had left after the introduction. "Before we're through we'll do a lot of hard smoking. Tell me about yourself. Married?"

"Yes, sir," replied the sergeant, producing pipe and tobacco. "Have two girls in their early teens. I was a senior constable stationed at Bathurst when the Superintendent was an inspector. That was eight years ago. The Super's been a good friend to me."

"He gave me the impression that he could be. During the period you've been stationed here how many homicide cases have you been engaged upon?"

"Not including these two cyanide cases, nine. Of those nine, only one was difficult to break open. You see, sir, here in Broken Hill we don't have gangster feuds, very few bashings, and rarerly a sex crime." Crome lit his pipe and tossed the spent match into the empty w.p.b. "Superintendent Pavier is the best senior officer we've ever had at Broken Hill. He's trained most of us, and he invented a system to identify characters reported from other centres. Every train and aircraft is met. Social evils which experience has proved everywhere cannot be stamped out are here quietly controlled, and, despite the surplus of males, our women are safer than in any city in Australia."

"What about petty offences—robberies?"

"Not much of that—until these last few months."

"Convictions?"

Crome's small grey eyes hardened. He hunted a purpose behind the bland eyes lazily looking at him.

"There's been four robberies this summer, sir. We wound up only one. The other three were done by an expert. Someone who's slipped into the Hill without our knowing him."

Bony made a note.

"What is your criminal investigation strength?"

"I'm the senior officer. Under me is Senior Detective Abbot and seven plain-clothes men. One of them is fingerprint expert and photographer and records clerk combined. Good man. Our laboratory work don't exist, but we depend on Dr. Hoadly, and without him we'd be sunk."

"Patrol cars?"

"Two. No two-way radio."

"H'm! Well, now, relax and tell me about these two poisoning cases."

"You know nothing about them?" Crome asked, plainly astonished.

"I've read the official summaries prepared by Inspector Stillman," Bony said, almost languidly. "Nothing of any value in them. You tell me."

Crome tried to keep the satisfaction from his eyes.

"Old Sam Goldspink was the first victim, and we didn't know he died of cyanide poisoning till eight hours after. Consequently the scene was all mussed up in the minds of the witnesses. It was on a Friday afternoon, our busiest afternoon of the week down Argent Street. One of the assistants took the old chap a cup of tea, and, as he was talking to a customer, he told her to put the cup on the counter. When the customer had gone old Sam took up his cup of tea, drank it, turned round, and threw a seven on the floor of his shop.

"The fact was that Goldspink was under his doctor for heart trouble, and Mrs. Robinov, the housekeeper, naturally thought that was the cause of death. When she was called, she emptied the shop, phoned the doctor, Dr. Whyte, and had the delivery man help her carry the body to a fitting-room at the rear. Dr. Whyte was up at the hospital with a midwifery case, and, knowing he couldn't do anything about old Sam Goldspink, he didn't hurry particularly.

"Meanwhile all the cups and things used for the tea and biscuits were washed up and put away. When the doctor did see the body he wasn't satisfied, and we didn't know anything was wrong till after the post-mortem that night. Didn't suspect murder. The old man had no

23

enemies; in fact, he was a bit of a character and well liked.

"When we knew it was cyanide, we got busy. The drill about the tea was this. Every afternoon at three Mrs. Robinov took a large pot of tea, milk, sugar, and biscuits to the fitting-room, and when the assistants had a chance to slip away they went there and helped themselves. Generally, the first one who managed to get away from serving took a cup of tea to the boss."

"Which one took him his tea that afternoon?"

"Girl named Shirley Andrews. Age seventeen. Been working for Goldspink for five months. Good character."

"What type of employer was he?"

"One of the best. Used to boast that his girls left him only to be married."

"When she put the tea-cup on the counter, how far was it from the customer?"

"Shirley Andrews says about a yard. The assistant serving the customer, girl named Mary Isaacs, says a yard and a half. They think in yards, you know. The customer was standing at the time, although she had sat on a chair when first she arrived and had to wait to be served. Goldspink was between her and the cup of tea. It couldn't have been the customer, but we worked like hell to find the woman."

"She never came forward? Did you advertise for her?"

"We did," replied Crome. "Same old tale—wouldn't be mixed up in a murder case."

"The public was informed it was murder?"

"Yes. Young Pavier saw to that. The Super's son. Reporter on the *Barrier Miner*."

"Pity. Were you able to obtain a description of the customer?"

"Yes, but not a good one. Both girls were a bit hazy about her."

"You searched the premises, of course?"

"Found no trace of cyanide. Only poison found was arsenic in cockroach powder. Check-up with the chemists gave nothing. Didn't expect it would. Have to sign for a minim of poison in Broken Hill, and can buy it by the pound in any of the surrounding townships. Tons of it used by the stations, you know."

"Well, back to the housekeeper."

"Mrs. Robinov! Been housekeeping for Sam Gold-spink for fifteen years. He left her all he had. She seems open and shut. Wasn't short of money."

"When was the will made?"

"Eight years ago. There are no relatives—no possible schemers."

"No mention of a codicil or a new will?"

"Not a squeak."

Bony gently worked to and fro his interlocked fingers, and Crome could not understand the smile of satisfaction.

"Interesting, Crome. The motive will be an unusual one—when we dig it out."

"Motive!" exploded the sergeant. "There isn't a motive. There can't be a motive, considering the killing of Pop Parsons in the same way."

"There's a motive all right. There is a motive even for me to light this cigarette. Tell me about Parsons."

"I made a hell of a boner about Parsons," Crome said, his voice abruptly savage. "I was caught right off balance when it happened. Parsons was a retired miner living with his in-laws. I'd known him for years. He had a small pension which ceased at his death. Big man who ate hearty and drank a little. He went into a café one Friday afternoon last December. The place was busy as usual. Sat opposite a man named Rogers, an accountant.

"Rogers says that Parsons—he didn't know him—asked for tea and sandwiches, and that he took his time over the meal, reading a *Digest*. He was still there when Rogers left, and Rogers says he thinks that then Parsons had eaten the sandwiches and had drunk one cup of tea.

"The tale is taken up by the waitress, a fool of a girl. She says there was quite a rush of customers at the time. She remembered Rogers, and she knew Parsons, who often went there on a Friday afternoon. When Rogers left, a woman took his place and ordered tea and cakes. The woman left when Parsons was still reading his magazine, and a second woman took her place opposite Parsons. This second woman was there when Persons drank his remaining tea, pulled a face, got up, and muttered something. She didn't take much interest in him, and the next time she saw him he was lying over the wreckage of a table—dead."

"The name of the second woman?"

"We don't know."

"Don't know!" echoed Bony. "But you inferred you obtained a statement from her."

"The statement is unsigned and undated. It was posted at the G.P.O. some time between nine and one the next morning."

"Your theory?"

"That on seeing Parsons sprawled across the table she

26

remained in the café to see what would happen, like many other curious people. She saw the proprietor rush out, and she saw the doctor and me come in. When she knew that Parsons was dead, she slipped away, determined not to be mixed up in the affair. Surprisin', the number of people who shy away from having to go into a witness box. Anyway, either her conscience persuaded her to write the statement or a husband or someone did. We advertised for her, but she never came forward like Rogers did."

"The woman who took Rogers's place—did she contact you or you her?"

Crome shook his head.

Bony made a note and Crome gnawed his lip.

"No motive suggests itself for this second murder?"

"Not one—only lunacy, and that's not a motive," replied Crome. "There was cyanide in Parsons's cup. I did have the intelligence to grab the cup. I should have —Oh, what's the bloody use?"

" 'It is folly to shiver over last year's snow,' as Whately or someone wrote." Bony stated with conviction. "You searched the café for traces of cyanide?"

"After me and Abbot finished with it you'd not recognise it for a café," answered the sergeant. "Not a trace. We looked for cyanide in and under and on the roof of the house where Parsons lived with his niece and her husband. Nothing. There was no discord in that home. Parsons hadn't any enemies. Never got a lead. Never got a lead in the Goldspink case, either."

"Ideas?"

"One. Lunatic going round dropping a pinch of cyanide into tea-cups. There's only one common

27

denominator in the two cases. Both men were bachelors. Makes the set-up all the more screwy."

"Makes it a little less 'screwy'," argued Bony. "There's another common denominator. Both men were elderly. They weren't friends, I suppose?"

"No. And they weren't related or belonged to the same club. One was a Jew, the other a Gentile. One was poor, the other rich. One had been a miner, the other a shopkeeper. They had nothing in common excepting age and single blessedness. There's no sense, reason, no anything."

"Do we get a cup of tea in this place?"

"Eh!" The expression of bewilderment on Crome's face caused Bony to chuckle. "Tea! Yes. The girl brings it round."

"If by a quarter to four we are not supplied with refreshment, Crome, we go out to a café. Without morning and afternoon tea, the civil servant cannot be civil. When a civil servant snarls at me, I say, silently, of course: 'What, no tea?'"

Crome stuffed tobacco into his pipe as though plugging a hole in a ship, and Bony went on softly:

"Homicide is a common occurence in any community, and we grow weary of stepping from the corpse to the murderer and showing him the utterly childish fool he is. But sometimes, and rarely, we are presented with a murder committed by an artist, and then all boredom created by the fool amateur is vanquished. It is so with this murderer of yours who pops a pinch of cyanide into a tea-cup. Why, we don't know. When we do know, we shall have to return to our amateurs who couldn't leave more clues if they sat up all night for a week thinking

28

them out. Surely this is an occasion for rejoicing. Have you ever met an artist in murder before? . . . No? Now that you most certainly will, you should be happy. I am."

Crome put his pipe on his desk. His face grew slowly purple. He muttered the great Australian expletive "Cripes!" and broke into a roar of laughter.

The Superintendent's secretary came in with a tray, and Bony rose to accept his cup of tea with a smile.

"Thank you. Miss Ball, isn't it?"

"Yes, sir."

The girl smiled at him shyly.

"The tea and biscuits will cost you two shillings a week, sir," she told Bony. "We can just manage on that."

"It's worth two pounds a week, Miss Ball," averred Bony, producing his contribution. "And we should all shell out every month for a present for you."

"Thank you, sir. I like to prepare the tea, but I'm only allowed to do it because Miss Lodding is away on sick leave."

The girl departed, and Bony dunked his biscuit. Crome said:

"The Lodding woman is the Super's secretary. Face like a stomach-ache."

CHAPTER FOUR

Jimmy Nimmo's Worries

Jimmy was still youthful, still casual about unimportant things, and a sportsman born with zest for the Game of Life, staking liberty against the jackpot and, having learned to respect his opponents, he seldom lost.

It was known officially that he never carried a weapon and never attempted violence when—rarely—he was cornered. It was also known officially, but never openly admitted, that Jimmy sometimes rendered valuable assistance to the police engaged with a major crime.

The amount of 'dough' he extracted from the Sydney bookmaker's flat was much greater than he had anticipated, but that had not been a factor in his choice of Broken Hill for a holiday. Like many thousands living in Australia's coastal cities, Jimmy had imagined Broken Hill to be a mullock dump far beyond a deceitful mirage, and actual contact with this city gave pleasurable surprise.

He found that lots of people in Broken Hill had lots of dough. He found, too, that the people of Broken Hill were extremely easy-going, generous, and affable. Strangely enough, they didn't seem to value dough. Wonderful place! Jimmy had plenty of dough, too, but he couldn't resist gathering a little more—without troubling to earn it in the bowels of the broken hill.

Now he was regretting it, for of a certainty Inspector Bonaparte would hear about those three jobs he had pulled and not possibly fail to stamp each one with the name of Nimmo. It was just stinking bad luck to run into him like that on Argent Street. He should have known that an ace detective would take up where that blasted Stillman left off, and that after two murders done the same way, Broken Hill was much too 'hot'—and nothing to do with the temperature.

To make matters still worse for a self-respecting burglar, this Napoleon Bonaparte was so damned unpredictable. He didn't tick like the common or garden flatfoot trained in a police school and taped by regulations and what not. There was that time during the war when he was living in Adelaide and had put through two slick jobs, and this Bonaparte bloke had come to his lodgings and said he knew all about those two jobs and suggested making a trilogy of it. The third job had netted a measly bundle of letters, but those letters had put two men and a woman behind barbed wire. Then Bonaparte had actually offered him honest toil. Jimmy shuddered.

And now Bonaparte was hinting at another spot of police work in these cyaniding cases when he didn't want anything to do with cyanide, he having acquired an important ambition since coming to Broken Hill. Fading out from this city to another would be just plain stupid, for the entire world was too small in which to escape the attentions of this cursed Bonaparte. Thus this feeling of the nut between steel crackers.

Arrayed in a light sports suit and a panama to keep

31

his head cool, Jimmy strolled down Argent Street. The afternoon was still and hot. The shadowed pavements were certainly not empty spaces, and the kerbs were lined by parked cars and utilities. The store windows were filled with luxury goods to meet the prosperity of this mining community, and the shoppers were dressed as expensively as he. Even then great wads of dough were coming up out of the earth to the accompaniment of the ceaseless racket of machinery.

The store once controlled by Samuel Goldspink was about the third best in Argent Street, and Jimmy paused to view the array of gents' ties and shirts. Ties! He already had dozens in various places, for he had an abiding passion for them, but Bonaparte had 'suggested' ties and—hell!

There were but a few customers within, and Jimmy came to anchor beside a man interested in gloves, and, there being a vacant chair, he perched himself on it with the air of a man having a million years in credit.

There were opened boxes of gloves on the counter before the man who was trying them on. He was a tall man, heavy, having a distinct paunch. He was very well dressed, even for Broken Hill. His voice was modulated and almost without accent. He could be a retired share-broker, an undertaker, a film producer. He could be—but Jimmy wasn't interested. Who would be interested in the man when one could gaze upon the assistant serving him?

She was barely forty, large, severely corseted within an expensive black frock. The pearl necklace floating on the sea of her bosom triumphed in the capture of Jimmy's attention, for they were real pearls. And those glittering blue diamonds set in the platinum rings on the fat fingers forced Jimmy's mind to envision the cot wherein these jewels would lie snug o' nights. There was certain to be a rear yard, with rooms opening to that yard. The burglar alarms, of course, would be just too easy.

That the wearer of the jewels might not detect in him a too absorbed interest in her trimmings, Jimmy casually watched the man trying on gloves. The hands were long-fingered. They were the hands of a gifted person: the hands of a surgeon, a watchmaker, a burglar. They were steady hands and strong, and Jimmy noted how the long and tapering fingers encased by fine suède curved inward to the palm to become a powerful fist whilst the owner examined the taut material about the knuckles.

So determined was Jimmy to ignore the pearls and the diamonds, he permitted too great an interest in the glove customer and suddenly was aware of being regarded by eyes almost black and decidedly speculative. It was just for an instant and created a fast picture in Jimmy's mind of a face adorned about the eyes with bushy grey eyebrows, and a grey moustache angled stiffly above a small goatee beard.

An assistant who had been serving a woman with a small boy came to serve Jimmy. Barely matured, she was dark and vivid. Jimmy was at once helpful.

"Ties, please, miss. Not too expensive. I like those in the window priced at fifteen and six."

To avoid looking at the pearls and diamonds, Jimmy glanced at the hand now being thrust into another glove, a brown kid glove. The girl was lifting boxes from the shelves behind the counter. The man was being fastidious. Gloves! No one wore gloves in Broken Hill unless going to a wedding—or a funeral.

Ah! A figured tie in pale blue silk. A little too dull, perhaps. A strip of light green opal caught the light as it wove about the assistant's fingers. Colourful, but certainly pleasing. Would go well with his newest lounge suit. Jimmy accepted the tie, angled its sheen to catch the light, placed it aside, and said it would do.

"This one is perfect for you, sir." the girl said, producing a 'creation' in red. She was being well trained by Pearls and Diamonds, for she exhibited interest in her customer. Jimmy smiled at her and placed the treasure against the cloth of his coat, agreeing that the colour scheme was perfect.

"I've a weakness for ties," he admitted, and the girl instantly smiled her understanding. "Now show me something less informal."

"I'll have that pair," said the glove buyer. "What price did you mention, madam?"

Jimmy blinked—once. The gloves chosen were black, and as the assistant folded them to slip into their cellophane envelope the diamonds sparkled yet more gloriously. The woman—Jimmy was confident that she was Mrs. Robinov, the late Sam Goldspink's housekeeper —appeared to be of a placid disposition, accepting the whims of her customers with fortitude.

His own assistant was displaying a tie which could be worn at a business conference. The glove purchaser departed, and Jimmy permitted a full minute to pass before remarking to Mrs. Robinov, who was replacing gloves into the respective boxes:

"You wouldn't sell many gloves in a town like this, would you?"

Mrs. Robinov smiled, and behold, there was a diamond in a front tooth.

"More often than you might think," she replied. "Mostly for weddings, of course, and for funerals. Generally a man wanting gloves is going down to Adelaide or over to Sydney. Much too hot up here for gloves—in the summer."

He was informed of his liability and passed a five-pound note. The girl accepted the money as though a gift to herself, and raced it along the overhead wire to the cashier.

"Are you staying for the races?" politely inquired Pearls and Diamonds.

"Yes, I think so," replied Jimmy. "I like Broken Hill, even in summer."

"I like it all the year round." The pearls gleamed as though seen through a fathom of tropical water. "I like the people. We're very sociable here in the Hill. I hope you have found us so."

"I have that," agreed Jimmy truthfully. Mrs. Robinov thanked him for his custom and turned to serve a youth who would doubtless have preferred the girl. Jimmy smiled at her on accepting his change, raised his hat, and sauntered out to the hot street.

His wrist watch said ten to four, and Jimmy thought of his throat and a pot of tea taken in accordance with the orders of that damned Bonaparte. He paused once to look at a display of new novels and finally entered Favalora's Café. The place was not crowded, and he chose a table against the wall. A waitress took his order for tea and toasted raisin bread, and Bony sat opposite him.

"Nice day," Bony said.

"Yes. Bit warm, though, for the time of the year. Might bring up rain. Does rain here sometimes, I heard."

The waitress brought Jimmy's tea and toast and Bony ordered the same. When she had gone, Bony asked casually:

"Are you aware that you are occupying the seat in which a man drank poisoned tea?"

"Yes. Are you aware that you occupy the chair taken that afternoon by the person who tossed a fistful of cyanide into the tea?"

"We're well placed. How was it done, Jimmy?"

"Simple. The victim was reading a magazine, remember? He wouldn't see."

"Why was it done?"

"Why? Just to watch the old bloke drink it up and throw a fit. Lots of peculiar types walking around, you know."

"If you wanted cyanide, d'you think you would have much difficulty in obtaining it?"

"Certainly not," replied Jimmy. "There's nothing I wanted I couldn't get—providin' I had the cash."

"Have you spotted the waitress who served Parsons that day?"

Jimmy sighed and looked at Bony with hurt-dog eyes. He waved his cup towards a girl waiting at one of the central tables.

"That's her," he said. "I'm taking her to the pictures tonight."

Covertly Bony examined the girl.

"My congratulations," he murmured, and Jimmy became really angry.

"Wasted," he snapped. "Youth to youth. I'm thirty-eight. My type wears genuine pearls round her fat neck and blue diamonds on her fat fingers. There's a burglar alarm to the front door, and no doubt other alarms are fixed to all the back windows. But what are burglar alarms to Love?"

"Mirages that vanish in the twilight," answered Bony. "Your girl friend doesn't look very intelligent. She sulked when Stillman questioned her. You know Stillman, of course?"

"The world's greatest living wonder."

"How so?"

"That he's lived so long."

"H'm! Let's get back to your lady friend. She will never be driven. She may possibly be led. A man and two women sat where I am that afternoon Parsons read his magazine and sipped tea. The man is out. The two women are of value. The first one left before Parsons drained his poisoned cup. She could have dropped the cyanide into it. The second one was seated where I am when Parsons did drain his cup and collapsed. She could have added cyanide to Parsons's cup. Pump your lady friend about those women. Lead her mind back to recall them, their age, clothes, mannerisms."

Jimmy groaned.

"I took her to the fight last night. All she did was to suck boiled sweets like water going down a sink and squeeze my hand like a dish-rag. And giggle! She'd giggle with a pint of cyanide in her. What do I get in return for all this agony?"

"No restitution of that Sydney bookmaker's ill-gotten gains," Bony said.

"Hell! You still rememberin' that?"

Bony nodded and poured tea.

"There are," he said, "many honest bookmakers. Perhaps you don't know that that particular bookmaker dabbles in blackmail."

"I do know, but that didn't worry me."

Bony smiled, and Jimmy's uneasiness increased.

"Regarding those jobs you put through here, three in number and totalling in cash and value six hundred and sixty-two pounds, I shall expect to receive restitution. Let me have the money in a neat parcel here to-morrow at the same time."

Jimmy looked wicked. The watching blue eyes blurred and their place was taken by a commodious two-storeyed house, not a mile away, which had become an exceptionally promising prospect. What he looked like losing on this Bonaparte roundabout he could pick up from that two-storeyed swing. He said quietly:

"That's a lot of money, Inspector."

"You must make a lot of money every year, Jimmy."

"About three thousand quid—on average."

"And no income tax. You can be lucky."

"I'm doubting it. All right, you win. What next?"

"I like your style, Jimmy," Bony conceded generously. "Honestly, I regret having to cramp you now and then. My investigation into these cyanide poisonings is going to extend me and I'm sure will provide you with fun and games. Continue to enjoy relaxation from business and don't worry concerning the future. You are the only man in Broken Hill versed in the highways and byways of crime and yet not a policeman. Who knows! I may want you to take a peep into a house or two before I'm through. I may even ask you to examine, among other objects, the treasures of your charming friend who wears ropes of pearls and hoops of diamonds. The sum you lifted from the bookmaker's flat that late Saturday evening was, I understand, just under three thousand."

"Bit over," Jimmy corrected.

"No matter. Do we play around?"

"We do," cheerfully replied Jimmy the Screwsman.

CHAPTER FIVE

Salvage

On leaving the café, Bony wended his way to the establishment of S. Goldspink, and, observing that the large woman wearing the pearl necklace was not engaged with a customer, he approached her and presented his card. Before she could read his name he drifted to the rear of the shop and became interested in floor coverings, and there she followed him and said coldly:

"Yes, Inspector?"

The dark brown eyes were hostile, the mouth grim. The pearls gleamed with automatism indicative of suppressed emotion in the ample bosom on which they rested.

"I am assuming that you are Mrs. Robinov," he said, brows slightly raised. She made acknowledgement by inclining her head, her expression unchanging. "Could we talk privately for a few moments?"

He was taken to what was obviously a fitting-room, for it contained a large cutting table, several chairs, three wall mirrors. Bony was not invited to be seated.

"I have been assigned the investigation into the death of Mr. Goldspink," Bony explained. "There is——"

Mrs. Robinov cut him short. Furious anger made her speak with emphatic deliberation.

"I am not going to answer your questions, and I am

not having my girls questioned, unless my solicitor is present. You can wait here while I telephone him."

"That would incur unnecessary expense," Bony said, faint horror in his voice and eyes. "Surely I don't look like an ogre? As you wish, of course, but why not put me on trial first? I'm not in the least suspecting that you or one of your assistants, had anything whatever to do with Mr. Goldspink's death."

"Inspector Stillman did," retorted Mrs. Robinov. "He nagged me almost to insanity and made Mary Isaacs a nervous wreck. I won't have any more of it."

"Inspector Stillman!" exclaimed Bony, and then vented a long and understanding "Oh!" Mrs. Robinov, who was actually on her way to the telephone, hesitated, turned fully to him. "Now I can understand your attitude, Mrs. Robinov—and sympathise with you. I'm sure you won't find me an Inspector Stillman. And I certainly wouldn't force my presence on you were it not for the fact that the person who poisoned Mr. Goldspink and Mr. Parsons hasn't yet been apprehended. It's all very unpleasant, I know. Don't you see, someone else may be similarly poisoned, and so I was hoping to have the help of everyone in the position to do so." Carefully placing emphasis on the first personal pronoun, he added: "Please don't think I am another Inspector Stillman."

The voice, the quiet assurance, the soft smile turned aside wrath.

"He is just a bullying beast," Mrs. Robinov declared. "We got along with Sergeant Crome all right, and Superintendent Pavier was always the gentleman. We didn't kill Mr. Goldspink. Everyone here loved him."

"That's what Sergeant Crome told me," Bony said soothingly, although Crome had said nothing of the kind. "Don't be afraid of me. I am sure we'll get along splendidly if you will give me the chance. You will?"

The hostility faded.

"Very well, Inspector. What do you want to ask me?"

"I don't want to ask you any questions today," he said. "But I do want to interview the assistant who was serving the customer when Mr. Goldspink was taken ill. Mary Isaacs is the girl, I think."

"May I be present?"

"If you wish, and will refrain from interrupting."

"I don't know. I think I should be. Inspector Stillman almost drove the girl crazy. I'll fetch her."

Bony thanked Mrs. Robinov and, when she had departed, he regarded himself in one of the long mirrors. He sauntered to the wall farthest from the entrance to the shop, and when Mrs. Robinov entered with Mary Isaacs, he advanced to greet them.

"Come along and sit down, and let's all be easy," he purred. "I'm happy to meet you, Miss Isaacs, and I am quite sure you are going to be happy to meet me."

He manœuvred them to sit facing the window light, with himself partially before it. He knew the girl's age to be eighteen. She was pretty and gave promise of becoming beautiful. Now her dark eyes were dilated with fear, and her lips were trembling, and he thought what a sublime fool Stillman was to think he could succeed with these women by the employment of methods he used on slum thugs and back-alley gunmen.

He spoke quietly, reassuringly, telling them he came from Brisbane, mentioning his wife, and proudly naming his boys and their achievements. He went on to stress the vital importance of 'catching' the person who killed Sam Goldspink and emphasised how silly it was for anyone to think they had had anything to do with murder. Gradually the fear subsided in the girl's eyes and the trembling of the lips ceased.

"Just relax, Miss Isaacs, and permit your mind to run freely," he said smilingly. "I've read all about you and what you said to Sergeant Crome and that other beastly policeman, and I just hate having to recall what must have become a bad dream."

"You needn't class Sergeant Crome with Inspector Stillman," Mary Isaacs said warmly. "Sergeant Crome's a pet. So's his wife. They live in our street."

"Ah! I stand reproved." The chuckle gained more for him than he thought. Mrs. Robinov, remembering the demands of her shop, rose to her feet, saying brightly:

"I must go. You listen to the Inspector, Mary, and tell him everything you can."

She smiled encouragingly at Mary Isaacs.

"Now tell me about Mr. Goldspink," Bony urged. "I know that he was shortish and stout and that he had a beard and hair still not entirely grey. Did he wear glasses, by the way?"

"Only when reading or writing," Mary replied. "Then he would sort of peer through them like looking through a telescope. He kept them in the top pocket of his waist-coat. Dragged them out and pushed them in so that it was a wonder they didn't break."

"I take it that his manner was quick."

"Yes. Quick in manner and quick in mind."

"Did he put on his glasses at any time when you were serving that customer with handkerchiefs?"

The dark eyes narrowed, and Bony patiently waited. "I can't remember."

"All right, don't try," Bony said hastily. "I don't want you to force your memory. One's mind is a queer thing, you know. It stores a lot away and is determined to keep most of what it stores. I've found often that the best way to make my memory work is to trick the old mind. I say to it: 'Well, if you want to sulk, go on sulking'. And then, when I'm thinking of something entirely different, what I want comes to me. Now tell me the routine of the shop—when Mr. Goldspink was here."

Every morning at eight a shopboy reported for work, and under the eye of Mr. Goldspink the boy would scatter damp sawdust on the floor and then sweep it into heaps to be carefully disposed of.

Dressed in an old brown velvet jacket, Goldspink would then dust the counters and chairs and be removing the dust covers when the assistants arrived at nine. Having opened the front door, he would check the change with the cashier in her office. The cashier? She occupied a small glassed-in compartment high up in one corner of the shop. Oh yes, she could see everything that went on in the shop.

There were few customers before ten, but the assistants were busy with their stock, and Mr. Goldspink breakfasted and then dressed for the day's business. His business clothes consisted of a frock-coat and black trousers. Yes, he always wore a waistcoat, a white or light-coloured fancy waistcoat. They were stained a little. The frock-coat was old but presentable enough. The black trousers needed pressing, but Mrs. Robinov probably had enough to do as it was. The boy always cleaned the shoes, and they seemed a little too big, but then Mr. Goldspink's feet wanted comfortable shoes to walk about in all day.

Most of all this Bony already knew, but he sat easily and nodded understandingly and for himself created the picture of an elderly merchant conducting his business. There had been no mention in any of the numerous reports he had scanned of the cashier's glassed-in office and its full view of the entire shop. She had never been questioned.

"I was told he was in quite good health that last day of his life," he murmured encouragingly.

"Oh yes, Inspector. I don't remember him ever being ill."

"Did he smoke?"

"I never saw him," replied Mary Isaacs. "Might have. I've seen him slipping a scented cachet into his mouth. Sometimes he lectured the girls about smoking too much during lunch time."

"They have their own lunchroom, I suppose?"

"Yes. Mrs. Robinov used to prepare the lunch. She still does."

"Did Mr. Goldspink have an irritating cough?"

"No."

"Or make a noise in his throat, as a habit, you know?"

"Oh no. Mr. Goldspink never did anything like that. There was nothing wrong about him, and he was always pleasant towards us as well as to the customers. He was very kind if one of the girls was sick. Sent her home in a taxi. And always gave us a bonus for extra-good sales."

"H'm! You know, Miss Isaacs, we're getting along famously." Bony stood and crossed to the large cutting table. "Let's play shops," he said, and whisked a costume dummy into place beside the table. "Come along. You stand on the other side of the table and serve the dummy with handkerchiefs. I'll be Mr. Goldspink."

A trifle hesitatingly Mary Isaacs accepted the suggestion, and then her eyes widened and began to dance as Bony pantomimed.

"We can recommend this line, madam. Been absent from the shops since shortly after the war broke out. Finest Irish lawn. Quality superlative. The best linen has always come to us from Ireland. You won't buy better in Broken Hill. Or down in Adelaide. Just look at the weave." He turned away from the dummy he had been addressing. "Thank you, miss." He whisked an envelope from a pocket and held it as though it were a cup-laden saucer, and the envelope he placed on the supposed counter to his right. To Mary Isaacs he said:

"That about where Mr. Goldspink put the tea?"

Mary moved the envelope. It was then immediately in front of Bony and less than thirty inches from the dummy. Bony proceeded:

"Yes, madam, the price is high. Everything is high these days. You have to be careful when shopping. Well, then, perhaps something less expensive. Miss, show the lady that new line in Australian handkerchiefs."

The assistant was now living in the past. Almost involuntarily she turned away from the imaginary counter to the imaginary shelves behind it and pretended to take from the shelves boxes containing the imaginary Australian handkerchiefs. She proceeded to open the

46

boxes and display their contents. Bony now turned slightly inward, away from the counter and the 'customer', towards the imaginary shop. The girl said:

"These are pretty, madam. The lace edge is sweet, isn't it?"

"Thank you, Miss Isaacs," Bony interrupted. "Excellent! Is that just what happened? Did Mr. Goldspink suggest that you display more handkerchiefs?"

"Yes. Yes, he did."

"And when you turned back from the shelves, was Mr. Goldspink standing like this, partly facing away from you?"

"Yes. I remember that he was."

"And the cup of tea was still on the counter—where the envelope is?"

"Oh yes. He didn't pick it up until after the customer had gone."

"And the customer was standing, like this dummy, when you turned round?"

"Yes."

"What was she doing?"

Crome had shot this question to her, and she failed to remember. Stillman had snarled it at her, and her frozen mind wouldn't give. Now, without hesitation, with natural freedom, she replied:

"Looking in her handbag for her purse. She bought three handkerchiefs and paid for them with the correct money."

"Did she take the money from the purse to pay for the hankies?"

"I don't think she did. No, she didn't. She had the money already in her hand."

47

"Which hand held the money?"

"Which . . . The hand—the left hand."

"The hand farthest from the cup of tea, eh?"

"Yes—the hand—farthest from the cup of tea."

"What was the amount of the purchase, d'you remember?"

"Ten shillings. She paid with a ten-shilling note."

"Well, Miss Isaacs, thank you very much," Bony said, genuinely delighted. "Come and sit down again. I won't bore you much longer."

They sat, and Mary said she wasn't a tiny bit bored.

"I wonder, now, would you know that woman again?" The girl shook her head.

"We know from what you have told us that she wasn't big like Mrs. Robinov, or short like—well, short. She was an elderly woman. You said she was taller than Mr. Goldspink. That right?"

"Yes, she was taller than Mr. Goldspink. She—she might have been taller than I thought. She seemed, now I come to think of it, to be slightly stooped. Seemed to peer at me as though looking over the top of spectacles. But she wasn't wearing glasses. I'm sure about that. I don't—— You see, Inspector, I didn't take much notice of her. I served thirty-seven customers that day. My docket book shows that."

"Thirty-seven!" echoed Bony. "Why, if I had served thirty-seven people, I wouldn't remember any one of them as a man, a woman, or a kangaroo. She was dressed in a grey frock, wasn't she?"

"I think so. Her hat was small, and it was grey or greyish. I've tried, Inspector, to remember that woman, but I can't. Even in bed, with the light out, I've tried to see her face. I have really——"

"Make me a promise. Will you?"

"Yes," assented the girl.

"Stop trying to remember. Promise?"

"Don't you want me to remember?" she asked, astonished.

"Yes, but not to try to remember. If you stop trying you will remember. Just forget about it."

"Yes. But——"

"You promised."

The dark eyes glistened. He thought for an instant she was going to cry, and he cut in with:

"Have you a sweetheart?"

The abrupt change of subject banished the danger, and the girl flushed charmingly and admitted to one.

"What does he do?" he asked, to give her time to regain poise.

"He works at Metter's, the grocer's. But he hopes to leave it one day and become an artist. He studies at the art school, and he's very clever. Sometimes they get him to do lightning sketches at a concert."

"An artist, eh?" Bony gazed over the girl's head and beyond the window. "Would he help us, d'you think?"

"He—— I think so—if I asked him to."

"Would he come to see me at the Western Mail Hotel to-night, say at eight?"

The chin jutted a mere fraction.

"I'll see that he does, Inspector."

CHAPTER SIX

The Art Patron

Bony was working in his office the next morning when his desk phone demanded attention. It was Superintendent Pavier.

"Morning, Bonaparte! Care to run in for a few minutes? I want to talk."

"Yes, all right, Super. Anything new on the board?"

"No."

"May I bring Crome?"

"Certainly."

Bony sighed and thoughtfully rolled a cigarette. If Pavier expected results thus early, if Pavier was to prove himself another 'boss' wanting a daily progress report, then he, Bony, would have to be firm. He lit the cigarette and pounded on the wall behind his chair. He heard Crome's chair being thrust back, and then Crome standing before his desk.

"The Chief wants to see us," Bony explained. "Have you found out who murdered Goldspink and Parsons?"

Sergeant Crome began to smile and froze it at birth.

"He gets that way sometimes," he said. "Me, I've got beyond worrying. I've had it. One of the girls is typing the report of your interrogation of Goldspink's cashier. You want it?"

"No. Let's go along."

Bony led Crome down the corridor, turned left at the junction, passed through the rear of the public office and into the room occupied by the Superintendent's secretary. He smiled at her and passed on to the door of Pavier's office and entered without knocking. Crome closed the door.

"Ah! Sit down, Bonaparte. And Sergeant Crome." The Superintendent indicated chairs. What was on his mind was concealed by the mask of a face, and there was nothing in his voice to betray his thoughts. The white hair crowning the long head toned out the colourless complexion. "How have you been getting on, Bonaparte."

"Oh, so-so," Bony replied. "I've been studying the groundwork done by Sergeant Crome and ruined by Inspector Stillman. I've been expecting another cyanide murder, but so far nothing of the kind has been reported. However, I remain hopeful."

This rocked Superintendent Pavier.

"I may misunderstand you, Bonaparte," he said coldly. "We certainly cannot permit another cyaniding in Broken Hill."

"I can see no way to avoid it, Super," Bony countered. "One successful murder begets another, and the second will beget a third. I wasn't here when the first was done, nor was I here when the second was committed. I have had to make myself *au fait* with the background of two murders, and for that I am given a fairly good survey by Sergeant Crome and witnesses whose minds have been blacked out by an arrant fool, a puny jumped-up would-be dictator, a conceited, empty-headed idiot of a man raised to a position of—But what's the use? You say you cannot have another cyaniding in Broken Hill. You should have said you would not have a second one, but you did. And you will have a third, because what trails were left of the first two have almost vanished beneath the clodhopping feet of the great Inspector Stillman."

Superintendent Pavier sat with his eyes closed.

"The two victims are beyond my interest, excepting to the extent that bodies are effects," Bony proceeded. "My interest is solely in the person who is the cause of the effects—two dead bodies to date, with a probable third in the near future."

Bony ceased, and Crome expelled caught breath. Pavier opened his eyes, and still his face and voice were without expression.

"It would seem, Bonaparte, that you misunderstood me," he said. "Being the officer in charge of this South-Western Police Division of New South Wales, I am amenable to public opinion. Hence my anxiety that a third murder will be prevented."

"I concede the point, sir. And when I declare that I am not in the least degree influenced by public opinion, that I don't care two hoots for public opinion, that all I do care about is hunting down a murderer, there need be no misunderstandings on either side.

"Actually, I am pleased that you called us in conference this morning. You will gain insight into our problem, and I hope you will convey these problems to your Sydney headquarters—with the suggestion that should there be a third murder, a fourth, or even a seventh, they will refrain from sending here any one of their several alleged detectives.

"Firstly, let us look at the scene of these two poisonings. A city deep in the bush, cut off by hundreds of miles of open bushland, a city made enormously rich by the world's demand for silver and lead and subsidiary metals. You have no gangsters here, no habitual criminals, no underworld, and because of that you have little need for a vice squad.

"Secondly, let us look at the murderer who drops cyanide into tea-cups. That person isn't concerned with vice or gambling. That person isn't a cracksman, an alley thug, a sex maniac in the real sense of the term. That person's motive isn't gain, jealousy, or anything so normal. Here in Broken Hill is a person influenced by a motive or motives which lie within the mind of the near insane.

"Thirdly, let us regard the two murders already committed. We know little of the victims. We know that both were unmarried, both were elderly, both were physically heavy men. Can we say that the person who murdered them is actuated by a phobia of bachelors, or of elderly men, or of fat men? As yet we cannot.

"And lastly, let us consider the investigator. He arrives on the scene precisely eight weeks after the second of the two murders. He is given nothing of any importance with which to begin his investigation. He is given a mass of conflicting reports and much senile theorising. He has to be unnaturally polite with witnesses made rampantly hostile, and he is forced to waste time in studying these otherwise helpful witnesses and employ expert psychology to bring them to the point of assistance. Given time, he may succeed in covering all the past police failures with the success of locating the murderer. I don't believe he will be given time to prevent a third murder, and that won't be his fault, nor will it be to his discredit."

The calm and precise voice stopped. Pavier shot a glance at Crome, but the sergeant was gazing stoically at his boots. Pavier was shocked less by Bony's assertions than by the justice of them. He saw the uselessness of treating this half-caste as a subordinate, and had sufficient sense to realise Crome's limitations and his own.

"Well, I was hoping for a crumb, but it appears I have to starve," he said, and after a pause permitted the hint of a smile, which swiftly vanished. "Speaking personally, if there should be a third murder, the public outcry will be terrific."

"Then the public must not know about it," calmly said Bony.

"Not know!" Crome burst out. "How in hell is the public to be prevented from knowing?"

"There are ways and means, Crome. First things first. The third murder hasn't been committed." Bony looked at the wall clock. "Ten past noon, and I've to see a man about a picture. You must excuse me, Super. I am a patron of the arts—among other things."

Crome stood stiffly, waiting for dismissal. Pavier faintly shrugged. Bony smiled at him and strode to the door. He left without the sergeant, and Pavier stared at his senior detective and again faintly shrugged.

"The only thing we can peg our hats on, Bill, is the fellow's reputation. Get out."

Bony passed into the public office and to the constable on duty asked if there was a Mr. Mills waiting to

54

see him. The constable called the name, and a young man who had been seated on a hard bench rose and came forward. Bony slipped under the counter flap to meet him.

"Sorry I wasn't able to call at your hotel last night, Inspector," the young man said nervously, and Bony told him to forget it, as Mary Isaacs had telephoned about his sick mother, and he expressed the hope that Mrs. Mills was much better.

"Come along to my office. I won't keep you long."

He sat Mills in the visitor's chair and produced a packet of cigarettes. Mills was perhaps a little older than nineteen, fair and fresh-complexioned, lean and alert and, as Bony was instantly to learn, modest.

"It's generous of you to come and see me, Mr. Mills, after the very bad impression made on Miss Isaacs by a detective we won't bother to mention," he began. "Miss Isaacs told me you are a lightning cartoonist. Would you work confidentially for me?"

"Yes, I'd be glad to," replied Mills. "I hope Mary didn't boost me too much, though. I still have a lot to learn and a lot of study ahead. If I can help, well, I'll do my best."

"There mightn't be much money for your work," Bony warned. "But you may eventually receive much helpful publicity. I am after the person who poisoned old Goldspink, and no one, not even your Mary, can identify him or her. We'll say it's a woman, but we must not talk about it—outside. Agreed?"

"Yes, sir, of course."

"Good! Take this sheet of paper and draw me."

Mills produced his own pencils from a top pocket and

fell to studying Bony's features, the point of a pencil poised above the paper. Then without his looking at the paper for a second, the pencil worked with incredible speed. The paper was passed back to Bony, who regarded it with astonishment and carefully placed it in a drawer, intending, on the instant, to have it framed and hung in his own study.

"I envy you your gift, Mr. Mills," he said, and meant it. "Have you done any colour painting, if that is the right term?"

"Water-colours. I'm studying that now."

"Excellent! Now I have here the description of a woman your Mary served that afternoon Goldspink was murdered. I have obtained the description partly from Mary and partly from the cashier. No other at the shop can help us. The details are vague, incomplete. I am hoping that with the limited details I can give you might be able to build, as it were, a picture of that woman. You will have to employ your imagination, perhaps make two or even three pictures, so that when shown to certain people, including Mary, they may assist those people to recognise the original. Will you try?"

"Certainly. What are the particulars?"

"The woman wore a grey suit and a grey felt hat having the brim turned up all round. She wore the hat straight—like a man wears a hat, not to one side. The hat had a pale blue band."

Bony waited for Mills to jot down these items before proceeding:

"The woman's face was neither thin nor fat. She was slightly above average height, and as she stooped a little she was probably well above average. She had the trick of inclining her face downward and peering as though used to looking above spectacles. Draw her with and without spectacles, if you will."

"Not much to go on," Mills observed, looking up from his notes.

"That's true. But do the best possible with what you have. Give me more than one full-length figure, and also a series of faces both full-face and profile. You may hit on just the right type to be identified."

"All right, sir. I'll do them to-night and let you have them first thing to-morrow."

"Thanks a lot, Mr. Mills. Grant me an added favour. Do not permit your Mary to see them. Leave that for me to do. Clear?"

"Certainly. I'll leave the sketches here for you at about eight in the morning. Glad to be helpful, sir. Rotten business, these cyanidings."

"Horrible." Bony rose and accompanied the young man to the outer office. "Not a word about this to anyone, remember."

"That'll be O.K., Inspector."

Mills departed. Luke Pavier appeared from nowhere and laid a restraining hand on Bony's arm.

"Anything of a break yet, Mr. Friend?" he asked, and the constable moved closer. Bony smiled and led the reporter to the public bench, where he invited him to be seated.

"Would you like to play on my side?" he asked.

"Sure. I'll team with anyone who'll play with me."

Bony steadily regarded Luke, the son of Louis.

"All set, I lead. You have my word for it that, if you

co-operate, you will be given the opportunity of being in at the arrest. My demands on you may, however, be heavy."

"Suits me, Mr. Friend."

"Good! Dine with me to-night?"

"I drink—a lot—with my dinner."

"At six. At my hotel."

They parted, Bony returning to his office and telephoning for lunch to be sent in to him. He worked until four and then went out and down Argent Street to Favalora's Café, where he enjoyed tea and toasted raisin bread with Jimmy the Screwsman. He returned at five and 'barged' into Superintendent Pavier's office.

"Hoped to catch you before you left, Super," he said, slipping into a chair and nursing a small package. "Often found it wise practice to rest the mind from a major investigation by indulging in a minor one. Kind of a busman's holiday. Felt I had to do something whilst waiting for what appears to be the inevitable third cyaniding. You have no objections?"

Pavier merely stared at him.

"On November tenth last year, the wife of a mine manager suffered the theft of jewellery which she valued at sixty-five pounds. The licensee of the Diggers' Rest swore that he lost four hundred and seventeen pounds from his safe on the night of December second. And a woman race-horse owner lost the sum of one hundred and eighty pounds from her cache inside her mantel clock sometime about January ninth.

"Those robberies were never cleared up, Crome tells me. Won't do, Super. Only encourages more burglaries. I have here the sum of six hundred and sixty-two pounds, being the recovery of the losses sustained. You might fix it up for me."

Pavier accepted the package, slit it open with a paper knife, and disclosed the packed wads of treasury notes.

"Make an arrest?" he asked quietly.

"Oh no. Couldn't do that. I never arrest a pal."

"Will you do me a favour?"

"Naturally."

"Come home to dinner with me to-night so that I can tell you in my own unfettered manner just what I damn well think of you."

"Another time, Super. This evening I am dining with your son."

CHAPTER SEVEN

At Morning Tea

The desk was littered with sketches of women. Among them were three full-length coloured drawings of a woman in a grey suit and wearing a small grey hat with the brim turned up all round. In each picture the face was different. There were several sheets of paper, each having half a dozen feminine faces presented at every angle, some with spectacles, many showing the eyes peering above the spectacles. David Mills had done an excellent job, and Bony was pleased, for in every sketch Mills had depicted the probable age of the possible poisoner.

There were three girls who might recognise in one of these sketches a living woman. They were Mary Isaacs, the cashier at the shop, and the waitress at Favalora's Café. If only one of those girls could say: "That picture is like the woman," then the entire police personnel could be put to hunt for her.

It was quarter to ten. Bony rang Switch and asked to be put through to Superintendent Pavier's secretary. Almost at once a strange voice said:

"Policewoman Lodding."

"Oh! Miss Lodding," Bony exclaimed, and mentioned his name and rank. "I haven't been presented to you. You have been away ill, I understand. May I come and talk to you?"

"Yes, sir."

Bony hung up, a quirk at his mouth. The voice was coldly efficient, not unlike Pavier's voice. Recalling Crome's impolite description of Policewoman Lodding, Bony left his office for her domain.

She was not quite as the sergeant had labelled her, and she stood as Bony approached her desk, flanked on one side by a typewriter and on the other by a card-index cabinet. In height she was above average, Bony estimated five feet eleven inches. Instead of uniform she was wearing a navy-blue pleated skirt and a tailored white blouse. Her hair, as black as Bony's, was dressed severely, which accentuated the sharp lines of the cheek-bones. The complexion was sallow, entirely unadorned. The mouth was not inviting, and the dark brown eyes held nothing akin to big velvety pansies. A female iceberg—aged forty winters.

"I am Inspector Bonaparte. Happy to meet you, Miss Lodding."

He smiled, with calculated attempt to melt the ice, and almost succeeded. She could not prevent the flash of interest in her eyes, and in that split second he thought he saw a different woman.

"Anything I can do for you, Inspector?"

"Well, yes, there is. Miss Ball told me that you prepared the morning and afternoon teas. That is so?"

Her voice was pleasing, and Bony waited for it.

"Very few young girls can make tea properly, sir. I generally do it."

"Well, the situation is this, Miss Lodding. I am going

to have a party this morning. Three young ladies from whom I am hoping to receive valuable assistance are calling on me. I want them to be perfectly at ease, to have no feeling of being within the clutches of the law."

"I could see to it, Inspector." The dark brows lowered a mere fraction. He thought they were hostile to his suggestion. They were not. "I'll have Miss Ball take in the tea when required. Having been away, I've a great deal of work to catch up on. You understand?"

"Quite. And thank you."

Policewoman Lodding made to sit down, and Bony, feeling a little chilled, left her. He found Senior Detective Abbot with Sergeant Crome and invited them to his office, where he showed them the sketches and explained their purpose.

"I assume there's an official car available?" he asked Crome.

" 'Fraid not, sir. One's being overhauled, the other's out."

The sergeant detected the hardening of the blue eyes.

"Hire a car," Bony ordered crisply. "Go with it to Goldspink's shop and fetch Mary Isaacs and June Way, the cashier. Be extremely tactful. I have a great liking for both those girls, and I won't have them being made nervous."

"What d'you think I am?" grumbled Crome.

"A policeman. You look like a policeman and you speak like one. Wholesome young women are not accustomed to being dragged by a policeman to a police station. I've already contacted Mrs. Robinov, who will give you her blessing. Now, Abbot, you go and get another car and call at Favalora's Café for Miss Lena

Martelli. Favalora will not oppose. Behave nicely. Rely on your personality. Bring those three young women to this office, and ask Miss Lodding to have them given morning tea. I'll see them individually. You, Crome, can be with me. Abbot can entertain them. Clear?"

Crome blinked, grinned. Abbot, a fair-haired man in his early thirties, chuckled. He was liking it. It was time someone stirred up this 'jug'. Who was to pay for the hired cars didn't matter just now.

In his own office, Bony rang Metter's Grocery Store and asked for Mr. Mills.

"Morning, Mills! Inspector Bonaparte speaking. Thank you so much for your sketches. They're splendid. Just what I wanted. You'd do more? . . . Good! By the way, d'you think you could obtain leave of absence for a couple of hours this morning?"

Mills said he thought he could, the manager being 'pretty decent'.

"Then come along as soon as you can. Bring a newspaper with you and wait patiently in the public office till I call for you."

Having instructed the duty constable to see that Mr. Mills was made comfortable, Bony fell again to studying the sketches. With clipping scissors he cut each sketch from the several sheets. There was a tiny smile at the corners of his mouth and a glistening of the deep blue eyes. Trying to find one woman in a city of twenty-eight thousand people, a woman no one could remember clearly, no one could positively describe . . . He couldn't even be certain that it was a woman who had dropped cyanide into two cups of tea. It could have been a man disguised as a woman.

An aboriginal tracker was told who to track. A blood-hound was given a piece of the hunted one's clothes to smell. To him they had given nothing of the poisoner save a few miserably vague details of age and dress. And then had the effrontery to expect results in five minutes. Hurry up, Bony, and catch this poisoner before he cyanides another elderly bachelor. We'll catch hell if you don't. And if he failed? Only scorn, only contempt for his mid-race. No longer any recognition of his achievements. For him one failure wiped out all successes: for the full-white, one success wiped out all failures.

"The girls are here, sir," announced Sergeant Crome.

"I'll see Mary Isaacs. Have Miss Ball bring her a cup of tea in here."

Crome vanished. Bony could hear feminine voices next door. There was the clop-clop of high-heeled shoes outside his door, and then he was smiling at Mary Isaacs and welcoming her. He was pleased that she smiled at him and then at Crome, who brought in a chair for himself.

"Your boy friend has done a great job for me, Miss Isaacs, and I have to thank you for persuading him to do it. All this is his work."

"He was a bit difficult at first, Inspector," Mary said, and flushed.

"But you managed him, eh? You women!" chuckled Crome, and Bony's estimation of the sergeant rose two pegs.

"Oh yes. You see, we hope to be married some day. And David's tremendously keen to get on."

"Well, he's gone quite a distance already," Bony told

her. "Now I want you to look at all these pictures and just see if any one of them reminds you of someone, and that customer in particular. Please don't hurry. I can understand why you are doubtful that if the customer should enter the shop again you wouldn't recognise her, so don't force your memory. Look at this coloured picture. It's a credit to your David."

The girl accepted the proffered water-colour and instantly exclaimed:

"This looks like Mrs. Jonas! Doesn't it, Mr. Crome?"

"Yes, something like her," Crome admitted, adding to Bony: "Mrs. Jonas is one of my neighbours."

"But it wasn't Mrs. Jonas who was the customer. I should have known if it was," declared Mary.

"Well, this one?"

The girl studied the second picture and then put it down, saying it didn't remind her of anyone. The sketches which followed were also discarded, and then one of a woman's face in profile puzzled her.

"Something like my aunt Lily," she said. "Not much, though."

Another sketch was thought to resemble Mrs. Robinov before she dressed for the shop. Crome sat beside her, keenly interested and yet saying nothing, giving her mind every chance to function.

Miss Ball came in with the morning tea, and Bony hastily cut off the work. They chatted over their cups, Mary telling them more of David's plans, of her hopes, and her work at the shop. Then the empty cups were pushed aside, and she was brought back to the task.

Again she looked over all the sketches, and finally she placed the three full-length water-colours side by side and gazed at them beneath a puzzled frown. Crome was silent. Bony barely moved. Memory! Was it being stirred to activity?

Mary Isaacs laughed, and, although disappointed, Bony delighted in the music of it.

"Of course! Now I see. Just what a man would do, isn't it? Draw pictures of a woman in outdoor clothes and not give her a handbag. You wait till I see him."

Bony almost spoke. He watched the vivid face drained of merriment, saw the dark eyes lose expression, and gain it. Her voice was so low that he barely caught the words.

"The handbag! I remember that woman's handbag. I remember noticing it when Mr. Goldspink was talking to her. Something red about it, and I hate red."

Bony waited. The girl stared at him, and then at Crome. Crome waited. After what appeared a long interval Bony asked:

"Can you now remember the customer's face, her clothes?"

Mary shook her head and then exclaimed:

"But I remember the handbag. I can see it now. It was a faded navy-blue suède bag with red leather drawstrings. It was squarish in shape. I've never seen one since that time Mother gave me a bag like it to play with when I was very little."

"What are drawstrings?" asked Bony.

"You pull them out to open the mouth of the bag, and you pull them close to shut it, and the strings become loops to carry the bag with. Oh, I remember that bag. I'd know it again. I'm sure I would."

"Well done, Miss Isaacs," Bony said warmly. "You

couldn't tell me anything about the customer's hands, I suppose."

"No. You see, she was wearing gloves."

"What type of gloves—colour?"

"They were like her bag, old-fashioned, navy-blue cotton," replied Mary, and Bony added to his notes. Without looking up he said:

"Crome, fetch Mr. Mills. He's waiting in the public office."

They sat, Bony and Mary, and each face bore a tiny smile of triumph. Youth looked at the man who seemed ageless, on whose dark countenance was not one line and in whose dark eyes gleamed dauntless courage that began before him and would live after him. And matured man looked upon youth with warm approval of human beauty and the spirit which bore it aloft like a banner.

Crome and Mills came, and Bony made the younger man sit at his place at the desk.

"I've been extremely careless, Mr. Mills," he said. "When giving you the particulars of the woman I omitted to tell you she had a handbag."

"Course she'd have a handbag, David," interposed Mary. "You should know. You've often enough asked why I carry one."

"I ought to have known." Mills was contrite. "I could paint one in easily enough."

"So I thought. The point is, when. Mary says the bag must be navy-blue, faded, with red drawstrings."

"Do it in a few minutes when I get home to my brushes and colours, Inspector," asserted the young man.

"You haven't dismissed that taxi, Crome?"

"No, sir. You told me to keep it."

"You go with Miss Isaacs and Mr. Mills in that taxi, and Mr. Mills at his home will paint in the handbag." Bony profusely thanked the artist, saying:

"Miss Mary will give you instructions about the bag. She'll tell you about the gloves I want you to put on the hands. I'd like both of you to promise not to say anything of this to anyone."

They were eager in their assurance, and Mills said they should be back before noon. Crome asked:

"Will you see the other girls, sir?"

"No, not till this afternoon. Have Abbot escort them back. Bring them again at three o'clock. And don't look at me as though you think me clever. I forgot about that handbag. And the gloves."

Bony sat again at his desk. He might have progressed farther than he was thinking. He might be given time enough to find that woman and discover cyanide in the blue handbag. The menace was real. It hung over Pavier like a ton weight suspended by a fine wire from the ceiling of his office. It kept Crome awake at night and ringed the man's eyes with red. It haunted Abbot despite his youth and small degree of responsibility. Café proprietors were worried by lack of custom, for men and women hadn't forgotten.

He slipped the residue of Mills's sketches into a drawer and drew to himself a writing-block. For a moment his pen hovered above the paper, then he wrote:

"To Sergeant Crome. Instruct all men in all branches to look for an elderly woman. Tall. Walks with slight stoop. Carries navy-blue handbag with red drawstring. Might be wearing grey suit, grey hat, and shabby navy cotton gloves." Then pen stopped, and Bony scowled. Now he was up against police procedure, that hateful thing which often balked him and which often he had spurned and triumphed over. If the bag was spotted, there might not be cyanide in it—when the arrest of the owner would create an uproar. He wrote, therefore: "Woman must be permitted to return to her place of abode that she be identified—unless identification obtained earlier. Important: woman's suspicions must not be aroused!"

Signing his name, he left the memo on Crome's desk and went out to walk up and down Argent Street. He could think clearer when in motion. How often had Time been his cherished ally? Time wasn't his ally now. Time was a Thing disguised as a human being who carried between thumb and forefinger a pinch of cyanide.

CHAPTER EIGHT

Three Gave Something

At one o'clock Bony returned to his office to find on his desk the latest edition of David Mills's work and a report from Sergeant Crome to the effect that the instruction concerning the woman and the handbag had been put into operation. Every policeman henceforth would be watching for the woman carrying that old-fashioned but distinctive receptacle.

Bony removed the string from the rolled drawings, back-rolled them to make them flat, and sighed his satisfaction. There were the three coloured pictures of the women, and in each she carried the navy-blue handbag with the red drawstrings. In one she held it under her arm; in the remaining two pictures she held it before her, open, her gloved hand inserted. In one of these pictures the woman gazed directly at the beholder, and in the other she held her head bent and peered as though above spectacles.

The handbag stood clear in perspective; the face, unknown even to Mary Isaacs, was less marked than the attitude of the figure. If the woman appeared on the streets with that bag and in that suit, no policeman could fail to recognise her, but if she appeared differently dressed and carrying a different handbag? Decided progress, but it was not decisive.

Abbot came in.

"You still want those girls on the mat, sir?" he asked.

Bony glanced at his watch and remembered that he had not eaten. He invited the detective to look at the pictures.

"I'll see those girls at three sharp, Abbot. Have these pictures pasted on to stiff cardboard and nailed to the wall of the general Detective Office. See to it that every man in the department is taken to study them. You've seen a copy of my instructions?"

"Yes, sir. It's already been duplicated and is being issued."

"Crome at lunch?"

"Yes, sir. Should be back at one-thirty."

"Inspector Hobson is, I think, in charge of the uniformed men?"

"That's so, sir."

"All right, Abbot. Have someone fetch me some sandwiches and a pot of tea, please."

Ten minutes later Bony heard Crome in the next office and he summoned him by thumping on the division wall. Informing the sergeant what he had ordered Abbot to do about the pictures, he asked:

"Your department on anything special?"

"No. Few routine jobs, that's all. Those pictures are good, eh?"

"Excellent. Think you could get Hobson?"

"Expect so."

Inspector Hobson was tall, lanky, stiff.

"I've already issued orders to all men coming on duty

71

to look at those drawings, Bonaparte, as well as to obey your instruction," he said in tones like breaking glass. "Happy to assist."

"Thanks. You can do more. How many of your men could you put temporarily into plain clothes without starving essential services?"

"A dozen," was the reply, with the proviso: "If for special duty."

"This is the situation." Bony took both men into the subject. "We're looking for a woman dressed something like the woman in the pictures and carrying a handbag faithfully portrayed in those pictures. The pictures represent the customer we think poisoned Goldspink. Of far greater value than the artist's colouring of the woman's clothes and the handbag is the woman's posture. People can change clothes and appendages but seldom are able to change walking mannerisms or posture. We fear that this woman will strike again, and for the third time in a public place, and therefore we must take every possible precaution to prevent a third poisoning.

"The danger is very real, for nothing begets murder like murder. I'd like to have a man stationed in every café and restaurant to watch for that woman, with especial emphasis on any woman who occupies a table at which is seated an unaccompanied elderly man of the type of Goldspink and Parsons. With the co-operation of the management of such places, your men could occupy an unobtrusive position.

"The woman, obviously, is exceptionally cunning. My instruction was that, should the woman be seen on the streets, she must be trailed to her home for identification, but if she is located in a café or restaurant, and seen to drop something into a man's cup or glass, she is to be instantly arrested and her handbag at all costs to be taken care of. The importance of these precautions outweighs any and all the results of a mistaken arrest."

Hobson stood without speaking when Bony finished. Crome waited on the Inspector. He knew that if the uniformed man objected he would get his way through Pavier, but he wanted to force nothing.

"All right, Bonaparte, we'll do that," Hobson agreed, having considered all the implications and all the possible effects. "With the help of Detective Office, I can have all those places policed by three o'clock this afternoon."

"Thank you Hobson," Bony said warmly. "That lifts a little of the weight."

"All in a day's work, Bonaparte. We're all in the same ship." A constable knocked, entered, and put a lunch tray on the desk. "You not lunched yet?"

"No," Bony replied. "Matter of fact, I had forgotten to."

"Well, we'll get going." Came a humourless grin. "Bet you an even fiver, Crome, that one of my men will nail that suspect."

"Do me," accepted Crome. "I'll back my boys till the cows come home."

They left Bony to his sandwiches, which he ate whilst pacing the width of his office. At three precisely, Abbot brought in the cashier at Goldspink's shop.

"Ah! Good afternoon, Miss Way. Take a seat," Bony invited the girl, or rather a woman, for she was nearing thirty, neatly dressed, and alert. Bony already had interviewed her and gained particulars of the customer's hat. "I want to take you along to see a picture of a woman which you may, in part, identify as the woman we want to question in regard to the death of Mr. Goldspink, and I would like to have your assurance that you will keep the matter entirely to yourself."

"You can rely on me, Inspector."

"I felt sure I could. Please come with me."

June Way was thoroughly enjoying this new experience. She was conducted almost ceremoniously along the corridors to the Detective Office. She met uniformed policemen who stood to attention to permit her and Bony to pass, and on entering the general Detective Office the group of men standing before one wall opened to allow her to view the three pictures. The men were silent, and she knew every one of them waited on her voice.

"The hat is just right," she said. "The woman stood like that as Mary served her and Mr. Goldspink talked to her."

"What of the handbag?" pressed Bony.

"I don't remember the handbag. I don't remember seeing it. I noticed the woman only when she was standing with her back to me. I didn't see her leave the shop. I'm sorry."

"There's no need for you to be, Miss Way," Bony said brightly. "You have confirmed the hat, you know. Thank you very much. The pictures do not bring to memory any other points? Take another look at them."

June Way tried, and gave it up. She had given to Bony the hat and woman's posture or carriage. Miss Isaacs had given the woman's posture and her handbag.

Now for Lena Martinelli, the waitress of Favalora's Café and the light o' love of Jimmy the Screwsman. Jimmy had done his best to provide the groundwork and had failed to turn the first sod.

Lena was fat and twenty. She was attired in a vivid blue skirt, a blood-red blouse, and a turbaned scarf confined her only beautiful gift from the gods—hair vividly dark gold. As Bony had not previously interviewed her, Abbot presented Miss Martelli.

"How do, Inspector. Pleased to meet ya. Wouldn't-a been lookin' forward to it only me boy fren' sorta put me wise—said you was a bit of a pin-up guy. I don't know nothing about that old bloke being bumped off, or remember the dames at his table. Help you if I could, sort of."

"I'm sure you would, Miss Martelli. And I wouldn't be surprised if it turns out that you can." Bony paused to offer a cigarette from the store he kept for offering. The girl crossed her nylon-covered legs and swung an expensive shoe, accepted his light, and looked into his eyes. Bony tossed away the burnt match and sat back.

"You remember the old gentleman who died in your café?"

"Who wouldn't?" Miss Martelli realistically shuddered. "You would, too, if you saw him spread on the table with broken cups and saucers and all the doings around him like a bloomin' salad. He'd been into our café a lotta times. I know 'im all right. Didn't think much of 'im, neither."

"Oh! Why?"

"Always sloppin' tea on the tablecloth. Had to change it for the next customer. Worse'n a pig."

75

"Did he slop tea on his clothes too?" Bony asked casually.

"Yes." The girl's mouth formed a *moue* of distaste. "Musta been a pig at home too. His old waistcoat oughta been burnt. No good in our 'ouse. We been brought up prop'ly, we have."

"Yes, of course. Well, I want to take you along to see some pictures of a woman we think may be one or other of those who sat at Mr. Parsons's table that afternoon. From the pictures you may recall to mind one of those women. You'll try?"

"Too right, Inspector. I'm all for law and order meself, as I told that swine Stillman a dozen times. The only fella who ever made me spit, the——"

"Let us forget unpleasant memories," smoothly interjected Bony, and moved to the door. "Come along. Oh, by the way, you would grant me a favour?"

"Sure. I'll take a risk."

Lena giggled, and Bony's sympathy immediately went out to poor Jimmy Nimmo. The giggle sizzled through him like a red-hot skewer.

"I'd like you to promise not to tell anyone about your visit here and what we've talked about. Will you?"

"Too right! Lena doesn't tell."

Bony was exceedingly doubtful, but he conducted Lena along the road taken by the decorous cashier. Lena smirked at those policemen they encountered in the corridors on the way to Artist Mills's exhibition and finally she stood before the pictures, blue eyes screwed intently, shifting from one foot to the other. As previously, Bony patiently waited.

"No, they don't hit nothing. Not a thing," Lena

said at last. "I'll bet a zac, though, that nothing like that woman sat at old Parsons's table the time he flopped. If either of them dames had a bag like that I'd have remembered. Couldn't forget it. Reminds me of a nappy bag."

"It's too bad, Miss Martelli," murmured Bony. "But never mind. I understand how busy you were that afternoon, and no one can expect the impossible. Is there anything else about that woman you would have remembered if she had sat at Parsons's table?"

"Yeah. Y'see the way she's standing—all bunched-up like? Me grandmother stands like that sometimes, and if that woman had been in the café that afternoon I'd have been reminded of me grandmother, see?"

"Yes, of course. Well, thank you very much. Mr. Abbot will take you back to the café, and I hope one day to pop in and have you serve me."

"Too right, Inspector. Tell me how you want your tea and it's all yours." Lena giggled again, and again Bony flinched. Abbot took charge of her. "Cheerio! Be seein' ya", was her exit line.

She had given nothing of the woman for whom alerted men now sought, but the interview had not been without profit.

CHAPTER NINE

At the Western Mail Hotel

It is beyond doubt that Wally Sloan is the most famous
man in Broken Hill and that his name will be remembered equally with those pioneers who discovered what
they called the Mullock Heap, which was to bring
Australia two hundred and fifty million sterling for its
ore.

Sloan is skinny, narrow-shouldered, slightly stooped.
He has a small but prominent paunch, gingery hair
fast turning grey, and a gingery moustache which
retains its pristine colour by constant contact with beer.
His eyes are pale blue and weak, his forehead that of
the intellectual, his nose that of the wowser, his chin
pointed and slightly receding. How old—no one knows.
And less than half a dozen are aware that he owns the
Western Mail Hotel.

When on this occasion Bony visited Broken Hill,
Wally Sloan had been at the Western Mail for nineteen
years. Yardman, barman, drink waiter, he is regarded
as an item of the furniture, the spirit of the lounge, a
permanent something of a hotel known to thousands of
visitors and spoken of reverently by stock- and station-
men and mining experts throughout this vast fifth con-
tinent. Familiar with all and yet withholding that
which makes familiarity objectionable, Wally Sloan

knows all the tricks to win the game from snobbery.

The public lounge at the Western Mail is tastefully furnished, and cooled by cunningly angled fans. Its main entrance is directly off Argent Street, and throughout the hot months the doors are always open. Chromium chairs are set four to a table, and during the morning and early afternoon there are the freedom and quiet of a club.

It was not the first time that Bony found it so, shortly before one o'clock, when luncheon was served, and this morning the place was empty when he slipped into a chair at a table near the tiny bar at which the steward obtained his orders. Two seconds later Sloan appeared, wearing a white drill tunic and black trousers, and coming to stand beside Bony and not before him.

"Sir!"

"Long lemon squash with the merest flavour of gin, please."

Sloan departed and silently returned with the frosted drink.

"A guest here, sir, aren't you?" he asked.

"I arrived recently. I may depart next week or next year."

"Yes, sir. You are Mr. Knapp, sir?"

"I am. I stayed here several years ago, when both of us were much younger, Sloan."

"Yes, sir."

The steward found it necessary to adjust unnecessarily a chair at a nearby table, and then turned, that for the first time he might examine this guest who claimed to have stayed here many years before. Bony's glass was empty.

"Again, sir?"

"Please—with much less gin."

"Yes, sir, certainly. You stayed here nine years ago, sir. Just for one night. Inspector Bonaparte, isn't it?"

"You have an excellent memory," Bony said approvingly. "Perhaps you would join me in a drink?"

"Yes, sir." The drinks were brought. "Your very good health, sir."

There wasn't the faintest indication of respect in the title which came at the end of almost every sentence. The sound resembled the staccato hiss of escaping steam. The word was a habit and required much less effort than 'mister'. A cloth draped over his arm, the hand of which held the empty tray, Sloan's expression was unaltered when he said:

"Hope you clear up our two cyanide murders, sir."

Bony turned slightly to gaze upward at the pale blue eyes.

"Someone been talking to you?" he asked.

"No, sir. I had no idea who you were until a moment ago. I'm glad to see you, sir. Your presence, sir, can have only one meaning."

"That's so," admitted Bony, adding: "I am Nemesis. I am he who dwelt in the mind of Victor Hugo and was born to the world as Javert. You would please me to remember that I am Mr. Knapp."

"Of course, sir."

Sloan made no attempt to move away, and casually Bony asked:

"What, in your opinion, would be the effect of another cyanide murder in Broken Hill?"

"Bad, sir, very bad. Yes indeed, the weather's hot but

not unusual at this time of the year. Mornin', gentle-men."

"Hullo, Wally! Mine's a long beer. Morning, Mr. Friend! Meet Mr. Makepiece," commanded Luke Pavier.

"Mine's a long beer too." said Mr. Makepiece before acknowledging the introduction. "Great day for drink-ing. How do?"

"Well, thank you. No gin, Sloan."

Sloan departed. Mr. Makepiece asserted that there was more beer consumed in Broken Hill on a Saturday than in Sydney in any one week. He was a huge man, perspiring and coatless. A waistcoat flapped against the sides of his enormous stomach. He wore no collar and his red face required shaving. He called for more beer before Sloan could unload his tray of filled glasses. He drank without swallowing, and Bony made quite sure about this phenomenon. He told two questionable stories, drank again without swallowing, complained he had to close up his shop, and departed.

"He's a butcher," Luke Pavier said. "Thought you'd like to see him. Has all it takes—bachelor, elderly, hearty eater and heavy drinker. You were about to say?"

"Nothing. Were you, Sloan?"

"Aloud! No, sir."

Sloan slipped away to serve a man accompanied by two women. On his return to the serving bar he heard Luke say:

"The last two happened on a Friday afternoon. To-day's Saturday. The last two happened late in the month. Next Friday will be late in this month."

Sloan repassed them with his filled tray and heard:
"You think your Mr. Makepiece is a likely prospect?"
"Don't you? Has all the makings. Only thing that
might save him is he doesn't drink tea in cafés or
stores."

The house gong throbbed announcing lunch, and
Sloan nodded to Luke as the reporter passed on his way
to the street. Bony he saw leaving the lounge by the
inner door, and five minutes later he was relieved by
another steward. Having lunched, at two o'clock he was
asleep in his room.

The Western Mail Hotel is a two-storeyed building
with a balcony above the street pavement. It is capable
of accommodating seventy guests, its bar and lounges
able to cater for twice that number, and the staff is of
necessity both numerous and well organised.

Saturday is the day of days when, there being no
work in the mines, the miners and their wives flock to
Argent Street: the women and children to drink tea
and eat cakes and ice creams in the cafés, and the men
to congregate in the bars and drink hard whilst listening
to radios blaring race descriptions. At the Western Mail
Hotel the Saturday-afternoon trade was fast and furious,
and the rush started at three o'clock. Extra barmen and
waiters were, therefore, employed to deal with this rush
period of the week.

Refreshed and wearing a clean drill tunic, Sloan went
on duty at three, taking charge of the public lounge and
a smaller apartment made available to the general public every Saturday. With the help of an assistant, he
served with machine-like smoothness about eighty people.

The noise was terrific and at four o'clock increased in

tempo. The blaring radios in all bars as well as in this main lounge, added to the din of voices raised in laughter and quip, upset bushmen in for a spree but had no effect upon Wally Sloan. Under or within the general uproar his mind registered orders and never failed, and he spoke to his customers, adding the 'sir' when addressing women as well as men, giving racing tips, and at the same time noting the broadcast finishes of races in Melbourne and Sydney or Adelaide in which he was financially interested.

Everyone knew Sloan, and everyone called him Wally. He seemed to know almost everyone and appeared to spend much time at each table for four, but no customer had long to wait for his glass to be replenished. His tables were set in four banks with the widest aisle in the centre, and he weaved and glided up and down these tables as though in this staccato confusion he was the only directed mechanism.

There were, however, unwritten laws which Sloan laid down and ruthlessly maintained. No customer was permitted to stand at the serving bar, beyond which two barmen co-operated with the two stewards. No two tables were permitted to be joined together, thus throwing out of gear the four banks of tables and reducing service speed. People were there to drink, and the staff was there to take the money, and in the background of all minds was the inevitable coming of six o'clock. When, therefore, six o'clock approached, decorum in drinking was sacrificed to the necessity of drinking as much as possible before the stupid moment when the Law said—shut up.

Among those who came in about four o'clock were

three men from Zinc Corporation. One was an engineer, another was a metallurgist, and the third was an under-manager. The fourth chair at their table remained vacant until it was sneaked away by a party at the next table who wished to increase their number by one.

Wally had known the three men for years, and he didn't bother to ask them what they were drinking. He carried long beers to them, talked for six seconds, took the money, and gave change from the coins on his tray. Many customers were as easy, for Sloan knew what they wanted and their wants never varied. Many of them were sufficiently considerate to have their money ready in a small pile on the table, that there need be no hindrance to a busy man. There were others who thought of money only when he set down the drinks, then dived into a deep pocket, changed their mind, pulled out a wallet, and then dithered before deciding to proffer a pound note or one for ten shillings.

Of these people women were the worst offenders, women unattended by male escorts. They kept Sloan idle whilst fumbling into handbags for change or purse, although well knowing the price of the drink they had ordered and that others waited.

There was one peculiarity about this Saturday-afternoon crowd which made it similar to the lesser crowd who came in on other afternoons. Certain people favoured certain tables, if able to get them. Parties of men chose tables nearest the main entrance, and un-attended women always gravitated to those tables farthest from the main entrance and nearest the small serving bar.

Round about half-past five there occurred another

phenomenon. Husbands drifted away to join their mates in the public bars, and the wives would look forlorn, then annoyed, and finally unite to refill tables. It always went like this, and Sloan could tell the time by the shift of balance. Thus at five-thirty, despite the approach of the awful hour of six, the lounges were less busy than at half-past four.

Shortly after five this afternoon two of the three men from the Zinc Corporation left, and the third man sat on, studying a plan which occupied most of his table. Now and then Sloan looked at this man's glass, and because it seemed that the man was so absorbed by his plan, he seldom bothered him.

At twenty minutes to six Sloan was standing at the serving bar, giving his orders to the barman, when abruptly the conversation at his back dwindled into a vacuity made the more emphatic by the uproar in the next lounge and the bars. On turning about, he saw the plan-student standing, facing towards the entrance, and then lean to one side, double, straighten and bend backwards, and cave in at the knees.

The serving barman thrust his head and shoulders through the opening above the counter. He saw Sloan run down the room snatch up an empty glass at a far table, and slam and lock the front doors. He saw the man stretched on the floor, sensed the significance of Sloan locking the entrance, turned and made a sign to the head barman, then vaulted into the lounge to guard the inner door leading to the smaller lounge and the back entrance. The head barman automatically ran out to the street and signalled a uniformed policeman stationed nearby.

CHAPTER TEN

Five Strange Women

Hans Gromberg, the metallurgist employed at Zinc
Corporation, died at twenty minutes to six. From that
moment no one was able to leave the lounge. At five
minutes to six Bony with Crome and Abbot and other
detectives entered by the rear door and took charge.

Familiar with the construction of the Western Mail
Hotel, Bony immediately had the smaller lounge cleared
of staff and the curious, and the customers, confined in
the larger lounge by the prompt action of Sloan and the
barman, transferred to it.

There were thirteen men and nineteen women, and
police procedure threatened to hamstring Bony. Abbot
and another man noted their names, addresses, and
occupations. Before this task was completed Dr. John
Hoadly had arrived and examined the body. To the
anxious Bony he said:

"Without an autopsy I can't be sure, but, just between
us, I think it's cyanide. Not for a million would I drink
the dregs in that glass someone said Sloan retrieved."

"Thanks, Doctor. We'll have the body in the morgue
under the hour. Would you examine it as soon after that
as possible?"

"Of course."

Bony's smile was wintry. The doctor was conducted through to the back of the building, and the photographer began his work. At a table in that corner near the serving counter Crome was taking down Sloan's statement, and Bony joined them and smoked a cigarette until the statement was concluded.

"Any leads?" Bony asked the sergeant.

"No, sir."

"People coming and going all the time, I suppose, Sloan?"

"Yes, sir."

"Well, we cannot keep these people here longer than absolutely necessary. Come with me."

Sloan and Crome accompanied Bony to the adjoining lounge, and there Bony asked the steward:

"How many present, do you know?"

Sloan looked over the small crowd and, to Bony's surprise, replied:

"Everyone, sir."

"Name them, please. Check, Abbot."

Without hesitation Sloan did so, and Bony then addressed them.

"Ladies and gentlemen, it's most regrettable that you should be present this afternoon when Mr. Hans Gromberg had a fatal seizure, and that what I am sure was a pleasant afternoon for all of you should be so tragically terminated. Now in view of the fact that it's remotely possible that Mr. Gromberg was poisoned, I am going to ask you to agree voluntarily to be searched before leaving. If Mr. Gromberg was poisoned, I am sure the poisoner isn't here, but you would greatly assist justice by eliminating yourselves from all suspicion. Obviously, if the dead man was poisoned, someone did it, and that someone was in the outer lounge at some time during the period Mr. Gromberg was there."

"Suits me," a man said, and a woman offered a sound suggestion: "Why not? Two of the barmaids could search us women. Good idea. Old Gromberg was a decent sort."

All agreed to submit to a search and, as Bony anticipated, not one grain of any poison was discovered. He had done all possible.

It was late when he dined, and when done he sought Sloan.

"Can you recall where your assistant was when Gromberg died?"

"He was serving in the little lounge, sir," Sloan replied. "He came into my lounge only to get the drinks from the serving counter."

"Then I won't bother him now. I'd like you to come along with me to Headquarters. Talk over matters in general."

"Certainly, sir. I'm only now beginning to sort things out. If old Gromberg was murdered, it's a ruddy shame. Good-hearted old bloke. Once a month he took lollies and books up to the kids at the hospital. Did it for years."

"Too bad. Let's go now."

Sloan was given a chair in Bony's office and asked to wait. Crome came in, saw Sloan, nodded. He said nothing when placing a document before the seated Bony.

"Too bad," Bony said, and Sloan noted the repeated remark. Bony returned the report. "Nothing from the uniformed branch?"

"No, sir. No fingerprints on the glass excepting those of Gromberg and another's. Expect they were made by Sloan. What about it, Sloan?"

"Take mine when you like."

"Ask the fingerprint man to come here," Bony said. "I want to keep Sloan's mind on the job. Draw up your chair, Sloan, and smoke if you want to. Have those pictures brought to me, Crome."

The desk phone burred, and a little impatiently Bony took up the receiver.

"That you, Bonaparte? Pavier here. Trot along for a minute, will you?"

"Very well, sir," replied Bony, and replaced the instrument with a sigh.

"In confidence, Sloan, it was poison—cyanide. When you leave here will you try and find Luke Pavier and persuade him to be as considerate as possible? He won't be far away. His father's worried sick."

"All right, I'll do that, Inspector. Known Luke since he came to the Hill as a kid. Smart lad, sir. Did right well at the Adelaide University. There's a lot of good in him."

"What's bad in him?"

"Cockiness, chiefly. Mother died ten years back. Sort of upset things." Sloan attempted a smile, adding: "Young Luke gave Inspector Stillman merry hell in his paper, and I suppose he couldn't help dragging in his father. I'll do what I can."

Bony nodded his thanks as the fingerprint expert entered and was left with Sloan whilst Bony went to see Superintendent Pavier.

At her desk sat Superintendent Pavier's secretary. It

was a quarter to nine. She was engrossed in a document, her forehead resting on the palm of her left hand, a pencil in her right. The fingers were working with a kind of nervous tension, and the pencil appeared to be sliding in and out among them like a snake among tree débris. At Bony's approach the woman looked up and the pencil vanished.

"You working late tonight, Miss Lodding?"

"Yes, sir. I still have a great deal to catch up with."

The dark eyes were brilliant, the face a dull white beneath the low-hung light. The voice was tired, but still pleasing to Bony, and she appeared so fatigued as to be ill.

"Better knock off," he advised smilingly. "Remember you've been sick."

For the second time Bony glimpsed the other woman, and he smiled again and went into Pavier's room. The Superintendent swung round in his chair to face him.

"Any leads?" he snapped out.

"No, Super. I have the drink waiter at my office now. Crome made his report to you?"

"Yes. You did right in persuading those people to be searched voluntarily."

"I can recall portions of police procedure," Bony admitted. "Still determined not to hush up this business?"

"Yes. Can't do anything else." Pavier looked as tired as Miss Lodding. "I must report the main facts to Sydney to-night. That'll mean an invasion again."

"That will be a pity—the invasion, I mean. Mess it all up. Delay me seriously, so seriously that most likely another unfortunate elderly man will be murdered. Better strongly recommend that poor old Bony be left in peace to finalise these cyanidings. You see, I have progressed. I do know why these three men were murdered."

"You do? Why?"

"My little secret. And I have one or two others. I am not sharing them with anyone from Sydney. I shall finalise these cases and hand them over to you all neatly tied up. I have still eight of the fourteen days allotted to me. I have all the assistance I need. No one here wants anyone from Sydney to cramp our style."

"Neither do I. Damn it, Bonaparte, I'm not complaining. I am only foreseeing."

"I know that, Super. In your report to-night, why not say you will be posting my report to you by the first airmail out? I'll flatten them. Now I must go back to work. All right?"

"Yes, Bonaparte, and good luck. We'll all need that."

At the door Bony stopped:

"I like your son, Super. We get along very well. More co-operative, in fact, than you have been regarding hushing up the cause of death."

"He has his job; I, mine. Been a good lad, but we've drifted apart somewhat."

"We can all drift two ways. See you later."

Bony said nothing to the secretary as he passed through her office, and back in his own he found Crome with Sloan. Crome had the pictures, and Bony set them on a shelf against the wall.

"Ever seen that woman, Sloan?"

The steward settled back in his chair and gazed at the pictures. Then he left his chair to stand nearer to them. On turning to Bony, he shook his head.

"Face is a bit misty, isn't it, sir?"

"Yes. Ever seen that handbag?"

Sloan turned to look at the pictures again, and again he shook his head.

"All right, let's forget the pictures. Stop fidgeting, Crome. Settle down and smoke, Sloan. Mentally relax. Gromberg and two men entered your lounge about four o'clock, and at twenty minutes to six Gromberg took up his half-emptied glass of beer and drank cyanide with it. You saw the person who added the poison to Gromberg's beer."

"Sir!" exclaimed the horrified Sloan.

"You served that person with a drink, probably more than one. According to your statement, you did not leave the lounge whilst Gromberg was there, so you must have seen his murderer. You assured me that you knew every man and woman who was in the lounge at the moment Gromberg drank his poisoned beer, and all those people consented to be searched and were searched for poison. Although we cannot be definite, we can assume that the poisoner left the lounge before Gromberg died. Tell me, and think clearly, when did you fill that glass of beer for Gromberg?"

Sloan took time and Bony waited. Crome sat motionless, contrasting this interrogation with those conducted by Inspector Stillman.

"I think," said Sloan, "I filled that glass about five twenty-five. It was nearer twenty past five than half past, anyway."

"Good! Now relax properly this time, Sloan, and re-create that lounge scene at twenty minutes after five. Let me help you. Gromberg sat alone at his table. He occupied a chair bordering the main aisle, to which he had his back. His table was nearest the entrance doors. At the table on his right sat two men and two women, until a third man removed a chair from Gromberg's table before Gromberg's two friends left the lounge. The two friends are out because you served Gromberg with beer at least once after they left. Now those five occupying the next table. What about them?"

"Regular customers, all of them. Two men with their wives. The odd man's wife was with another party. The five were included with those searched."

"When Gromberg died, all the people present you vouched for. About how many people in the lounge were there you couldn't have vouched for when you served Gromberg with his last drink? Don't hurry."

There was a tap on the door, and Bony motioned to Crome to attend to it. Crome spoke with a man in the corridor, came back and placed a report on the desk. Sloan sat with his eyes closed. Bony read:

"Fingerprints on the glass those of the dead man and Walter Sloan."

Sloan coughed and Bony looked up. The steward's eyes were open. He said:

"I can't be sure about the number. The place wasn't as full as it was half an hour before, some of the men having left for the public bars. There was a party of two men and two women at a table halfway from the front entrance, and several women right back at my end who I don't remember seeing before."

"Unattended women?"

"Yes. They seem to like getting as far from the front entrance as possible. I don't know why."

"Those several women left before Gromberg died?"

"Must have done. They weren't there when he died."

"And when leaving they passed close behind Gromberg?"

"Yes. They'd have to, to reach the front door."

"Concentrate on them. Did a woman stop, or pause in her progress, at Gromberg's chair?"

"I didn't see one, sir," replied Sloan, and the return of the 'handle' indicated returning confidence. "Just a minute, sir."

Silence, and Bony and Crome waited. Sloan again studied the coloured drawings.

"No, I don't know her,' Sloan said. "Never saw her. Unattended women! There were a dozen of 'em, at least. Add them I knew. Two married women. Three respectable molls. A widow who used to be a barmaid. Woman who runs a frock shop. And a single woman I don't know what she does. How many's that?"

"Eight," replied Crome.

"That—— There was Mrs. Lance, that makes nine. There were five unescorted women I didn't know. Yes, five."

"Was one of those five fairly tall, average weight, dark eyes, wearing glasses?"

"Don't remember. Don't think so, sir. There was a big woman, grey hair, face like a clock at twenty to four. Drank brandy—neat. There was one all dolled up to kill, kept fiddling with her handbag, wasting my time as she dug out the price of her drinks."

"That leaves three, Sloan," murmured Bony. "Concentrate on them. Did one of them wear glasses and look over them at you?"

"No. One was youngish. Drank gin and water—silly fool, at her age. Another time-waster was about fortyish. Dolled up too. She drank ginger ale. And the other was an old dame, short and fat and beery."

"The time-waster about fortyish. You mean she, too, doodled with the money?"

"Yes. Drank ginger ale."

"That unusual?"

" 'Course, sir. Why go to a pub to drink rotgut all by yourself? Cafés are the places for that. Women call for soft drinks in a pub when they're with a husband or man friend."

"And this one was all dressed up?"

"Yes, sir. Plenty of powder and paint. Fairly well dressed, I think. Blue and white, and a white hat."

"Handbag?" prompted Bony.

"Handbag!" Sloan frowned. "Don't remember. Too many handbags around. Damned nuisance, littering up the tables when I want to set down drinks."

"Does a blue handbag with red handles register?" pressed Bony.

"No." Sloan was decidedly despondent. And then he brightened. "I'll tell you what, sir. Mrs. Wallace, who used to be a barmaid, might remember. She sat next to the woman in the bue and white dress."

"An idea, Sloan. Mrs. Wallace! D'you know where she lives?"

Sloan did know, and Crome noted the address, and also the addresses of several of the other women Sloan knew.

"Just where did she sit, the woman in the blue and white dress?" Bony went on.

95

"With her back to the rear wall, sir."

"She could see Gromberg all the time?"

"Yes. She went out . . . I remember now. She left after Mrs. Wallace did. She went just before I was asked for four double whiskies. I was waiting for the whiskies at the service bar, when people stopped talking and I turned round to see Gromberg pass out."

Knowing the wisdom of not tiring a witness, Bony stood up and dismissed the steward, saying:

"You have done remarkably well, Sloan."

CHAPTER ELEVEN

Sunday

"What's to be our next move?" Bony asked, when Sloan had gone. The sergeant had pushed his notes aside and was loading his pipe.

"Concentrate on those unescorted women. One of them must have done it."

"We'll winnow, Crome. There were four tables at which sat sixteen people—fourteen women and two men. Sloan knew the two men and nine women. We have their names and addresses. The remaining five women were not known to Sloan, so we will concentrate on them. Or rather I will, because you and your men have much to do. Leave Mrs. Wallace to me.

"I'm sorry to push the routine work on to you, but it must be done. Being Saturday and already late, and many people at the cinema, we'll both start in earnest in the morning. You check up on those people known to Sloan, with the exception of Mrs. Wallace, ask if they remember a woman with a blue handbag having red drawstrings, and at the same time get their background. You may find a lead connecting them with either Goldspink or Parsons."

"Seems the next move," agreed Crome.

"Then on Monday put your gang on to all chemists

97

and wholesale stores and check up on their sales of cyanide. It was done before, but it must be done again. You yourself, visit every mine where cyanide is used in the extraction of gold or for other purposes, and check on that source of supply. You sent Abbot to fine-comb Gromberg's house?"

"Yes, sir. Ought soon to be back."

"I'm reminded that I have to send a report through the Super to Sydney. Must avoid interference. Don't permit the public reaction to worry you. The Super is the man to take all that. It's what he's paid for. Your job, and mine, is to unearth this poisoner."

"Be less worrying if we could get a clear lead," grumbled Crome.

"We have several leads."

"Well, that blue handbag with red strings can't be called——"

"The good investigator deals with items, such as that handbag. Through them he can understand the quarry's motives and uncover his identity.

"This unfortunate Hans Gromberg is a part of what is now certain to be a pattern. He was a bachelor. He was elderly. He was a robust eater and a hard drinker. Like Goldspink, but unlike Parsons, he was a generous man. Are those three victims high lights of the pattern because they were unmarried, or because they were elderly, or because they were elderly bachelors, or because they were robust, or careless feeders? Or did each one of them represent a hated figure of one man?"

"What's careless eating got to do with it?" asked Crome. "A dried-up spinster could go barmy and have a dead set against old bachelors. Read of a case like that some time or other."

"What is your reaction to the man who slops his food and his front is stained and greasy?"

"Disgust."

"How much more so would an elderly spinster be disgusted?"

"Then you think the three common factors make a picture of the three murder victims as one, in a mind hating like hell?"

"That is what I am inclined to think," answered Bony. "The shop assistant told me that Goldspink's waistcoat was food-stained. The waitress told me that Parsons's clothes were stained with food. And I saw that the waistcoat worn by Gromberg was similarly soiled. So you see—we have progressed."

"Then we have to look for a ratty old maid?"

"Yes and no. I feel that we can be confident that the poisoner is a woman. We may, of course, have to alter these theories. We can find no link between Goldspink and Parsons, but we may discover a link between Gromberg and Goldspink or Parsons. Mrs. Robinov benefited from Goldspink's death, but no one did from Parsons's death. As illustration: should we find that Mrs. Robinov is to benefit under Gromberg's will, then we would with reason assume that she is clever enough to have poisoned old Parsons to make the motive appear as though emanating from the brain of a near-insane woman—which she is not. In history there has been a series of murders done to hide the motive for killing a particular person."

The sergeant pounced.

"Near insane?" he exclaimed. "Can anyone be near insane?"

"Oh yes, Crome, yes, of course. Our asylums are full of the partially insane. Some never enter an asylum, not being ill enough and their relatives willing to care for them. Others fall into a distinct category. They suffer from what is called progressive insanity, eventually compelling the authorities to certify and confine. Of all the ills to which mankind is subject, initial insanity is the hardest to detect.

"I'll go back one step. If through Gromberg's murder we find that greed, or jealousy, or ambition is the motive, then we look for a sane and clever murderer. If, on the other hand, Gromberg's murder links in no one respect with those of the others to give us a motive, then we must look for the near-insane person possessed of intense hatred of elderly, slovenly bachelors."

Crome sighed. Seriously he said:

"Well, I'm just an ordinary ruddy policeman. I can pinch drunks and keep vice in check. Stillman's another policeman. He can wage war with gunmen and pinch men who cut the wife's throat because she nags, or is mucking about with another man, or because he wants a clear field to marry another woman. I can deal with those sorts of murders too. When it comes to these near-insane killings, I'm stonkered. And so's Stillman and the Super."

The tacit admission did more for Bony than Crome was ever to know.

"One must be patient and refuse to be sidetracked," Bony said. "And now I must write my report for the Super. You go home to bed."

"Can't. Must wait to see what Abbot brings in."

Crome left the room and Bony brought his mind to composing his report, knowing that to achieve freedom of action he would have to write in a manner divorced from his verbal bouts with superiors. The task occupied him an hour, and on his way out to return to his hotel he met Crome again.

"Abbot found nothing like poison in Gromberg's house," he told Bony. "He did find a set of diaries, and he read back for the last six months and couldn't find a link with either Parsons or Goldspink. Found a will, too, dated a year ago. The will leaves everything to a nephew in New Zealand. Doesn't say how much."

"Thanks! Put a man on routine investigation into Gromberg's background. I'm going to bed."

It was not particularly late when Bony turned in, but he slept till nine next morning, then rang for Sloan, asking the steward to be generous and fetch him a breakfast tray. It was eleven when he left the hotel and, without difficulty, found a taxi.

Sunday morning, and Argent Street deserted save for men supporting veranda posts, some of them having coursing dogs in leash and most of them talking sport. The famous street was silent, and the silence was emphasised by noise of the mine machinery which, although reduced, never stops.

The car carried Bony down Argent Street, turned to cross the railway and pass the Trades Hall, where so much of local history has been made, turned again to skirt one of the two railway terminals, and proceeded along what was formerly a low ridge, enabling Bony to see the broken hill and what man had done to it.

Even the brazen sky looked Sundayish, and the spiralling smoke and spurting steam about the mine heads pretended to be taking this day off—or wanting to.

Finally the taxi stopped before a small house set close behind a peeling picket fence. The driver was asked to wait, and Bony passed through where once a gate had been, and mounted two steps to the front door.

In answer to his knock the door was opened by a girl of school age, who said her mother was at home. She left him standing at the open doorway, and he heard her shouting:

"Hi, Mum, a gent wants to see you."

A woman's voice: "Blast! Tell him to wait. I ain't dressed yet. What's he look like?"

"A-ah, just a man. Got his best clothes on."

As though this conversation could not possibly have reached the caller, the girl reappeared, to say that her mother wouldn't be long. Again the deserted Bony stood on the porch, this time for ten minutes, when a figure in a voluminous house-gown of lollipop-pink confronted him.

"Pardon my disarray," she said genteelly. "Hate being rushed on a Sunday morning. What is it?"

"I'm from the Detective Office, Mrs. Wallace. Wally Sloan told me you might be in a position to help us in a certain matter."

Mrs. Wallace was fifty, amazingly blondish, and her hastily applied 'Morning-Glory' make-up was somewhat misty.

"Blimey! You don't say," she said. "Come in." Bony

was taken to the front parlour, a place of signed photographs, bric-à-brac, cushions, and a velvet lounge suite. "Right about Gromberg, then?"

"You have heard?"

"That old Gromberg died in the Western Mail, sudden-like? What did he die of—Mr.—Sergeant—Inspector?"

"Inspector. Mr. Gromberg died of cyanide."

"You don't say!" Mrs. Wallace settled herself comfortably. This was going to be good—not to be hurried. She lifted up her voice and screamed: "El-sie!"

"Yes, Mum!" shouted the girl from somewhere at the rear.

"You made that coffee yet, luv?"

"Yes. You want it now?"

"What'd you think? Bring an extra cup for the gentleman." To Bony she said placidly: "Getting serious, isn't it?"

"The poisonings, yes. Sloan told me that you left the lounge at the Western Mail Hotel only a few minutes before Gromberg took up his glass of beer, drank it, and immediately died. The glass had last been filled about twenty minutes past five and he emptied it at twenty minutes to six. You left, as far as Sloan remembers, at five and twenty to six."

"Yes, it was about half-past five." Mrs. Wallace raised a hand to warn him of the approach of the girl. Self-consciously she carried a silver-plated tray covered with a lace cloth and bearing cups and saucers, sugar, hot milk, and a coffee pot. The mother swept knick-knacks off a small table to make room for the tray, and the girl departed. Mrs. Wallace then produced a bottle of brandy, smiled at Bony, poured a liberal portion into one cup, and presented him with the bottle.

"All yours," she told him. "Went to a 'do' last night. Got an awful itchy throat."

Bony voiced appreciation of the coffee but declined the brandy.

"Where you sat in the lounge you could see everyone and watch everyone entering and leaving, couldn't you?"

"You bet," agreed Mrs. Wallace. "I like lookin' at people."

"Do you often spend a few minutes there?"

Mrs. Wallace chuckled, and the bosom reminded Bony of the groundwork of Mrs. Robinov's pearls.

"More like a couple of hours, Inspector. I go there most Satdee afternoons. Only little pleasure I get these days. Used to work in a bar one time, y'know. I like the atmosphere."

"It's because you are used to bars and lounges that I am hoping you can give me one or two pointers." Bony sipped his coffee. "The little girl can certainly brew coffee."

"Too right, I'm teaching her to be refined. Sing out when you want another cuppa. You was sayin'?"

"On leaving your table for the front door, you had to pass behind Mr. Gromberg, didn't you?"

"I had to, yes."

"Did you notice how much beer was then in his glass?"

"I fancy I did. Being a barmaid, I can tell beer at a glance, and you've sorta brought it to my mind. Gromberg's glass, I'd say, was a bit over half full. I remember thinking as I walked out that the beer served to Gromberg was a bit off, and I couldn't get it because my beers had been O.K. The beer in Gromberg's glass was cloudy, and I said to meself in the street that it was the first time I'd seen cloudy beer at the Western Mail."

The woman's eyes grew small, and her large mouth pursed in an expression of genuine horror.

"That cloudiness! You don't think——"

"And don't you, Mrs. Wallace," Bony urged. "Let's have these times straight. Wally Sloan last filled Mr. Gromberg's glass at about twenty past five, and you left the lounge at twenty-five to six. Can you remember who left after twenty past five and before you did?"

Mrs. Wallace frowned as though Bony had made an indelicate remark. She continued to frown as she filled Bony's cup and added brandy to her own.

"Several people went out—mostly women from my end of the lounge. The party next to me left just before I did."

"Did you happen to see these people pass Mr. Gromberg? They would all have to pass at his back, wouldn't they?"

"They'd all have to do that, the way he was sitting. I'd seen some of 'em there before yesterdee. That's funny! The party sitting next to me was a queer one. I spoke to her twice, and she never said nothing, so I didn't bother. Drank ginger ale, too. First of all I thought she was there waiting for a man to turn up. Then I reckoned that couldn't be as she wasn't the sort to be waiting anywhere for a man."

"Can you recall if she passed particularly close to Mr. Gromberg?"

"No closer than need be," replied Mrs. Wallace. "I thought she knew the woman sitting my side of Gromberg and with her back to the passageway. Just as she got to this woman she put out her hand as if she was going to touch her, then sorta altered her mind and went on past Gromberg. She never put her hand near Gromberg's glass. I'd swear to that."

"Just now you said this woman was a queer one. What was queer about her?"

"Well, she drank ginger ale in a pub lounge, for one thing. There was another thing. She didn't want to talk to me—not that I pressed her. Them that's independent can be, far as I'm concerned. Looked to me like she'd never been in a pub before and was expectin' to meet the devil any time.

"Old-maidish. You know, you can tell 'em. She didn't wear a weddin' ring, but that's neither here nor there these days. This one was about fifty and got up to be thirty. Some of 'em are pretty good at it, but they don't pull no wool over May's eyes.

"Then there was her handbag. Kept it on her lap all the time and fumbled to get at her purse, and Wally waiting for his money and people yelling for more drinks. Once she nearly knocked her ginger ale all over her dress, what she mustar kept in lavender. It was blue and white, and I haven't seen that sorta silk for years. And do you know what I got a peep of in her handbag? I'll tell you. It was a baby's dummy."

"A baby's dummy!" echoed Bony.

"A baby's dummy. I seen the thing, I tell you. Pale brown rubber teat like beer. I hate 'em. Never give my kids them filthy things. Poor little mites. They trail all over the floor, with the cat playing with 'em and the dog licking 'em. And then the fond mother picking it up and stuffing it back into the little rosebud of a mouth —flies, dirt, spit, and all. The only thing a baby should have to suck is a good big clean mutton bone. No meat on it, of course—not at the start."

"What kind of handbag was it?" came the inevitable question.

"Handbag! Blue, I think. The old drawstring sort. Red drawstrings they was. Now what would a baby's dummy be doing in a virgin's handbag? You tell me that, Inspector."

As Mrs. Wallace expected an answer, Bony murmured:

"It's beyond me. Would you know the woman again?"

"I certainly would."

"Excuse me for a moment. I'll show you some pictures I have out in the taxi." He was back under the minute, and Mrs. Wallace looked at Artist Mills's work and slowly shook her head.

"No, she wasn't anything like them women," she said in a manner precluding any doubt. "The handbag looks like the one, though."

CHAPTER TWELVE

The Hidden Woman

On this Sunday afternoon Bony walked with Wally Sloan to the man-made crater top of the broken hill and looked down upon the city courting the fabulous line of lode fashioned by chance to the shape of a giant boomerang. The sun was yellow in a cadmium sky, and beyond the jumble of the tree-denuded Barrier Range the celestial dome imprisoned ghostly clouds.

They sat on a pile of hardwood, and Sloan, having regained his wind was inclined to talk, and because he wanted to rest his mind from its many problems Bony was satisfied to let him talk about Broken Hill. At their feet, beyond the narrow flat, ran the centre of the city —Argent Street—and away to the southward the populous suburb of South Broken Hill sprawled like a great mass of conglomerate upon the vast plain stretching away to the Murray River.

Sloan related the story of how the original syndicate raised new money by creating fourteen equal shares, and how a game of euchre decided the sale of one of these shares for £120. Had this share remained intact, within six years it would have been worth £1,250,000.

"That's money," Sloan said. "You didn't want faith, and you didn't want vision. All you had to have was luck—just to hold on to something you thought worth-less. Now look at her. She isn't big, but she's got the doings, that little city of ours. The state and federal governments draw twelve million quid a year out of her, and still she has to have everything of the best from beer to refrigerators.

"She's a healthy city, too, a long way different to the times when the smelters were here. Men used to be walking home, or going to work, and drop in their tracks in a kind of fit, and when it rained good and heavy and made the street gutters run, the poisons from the mines killed cats and dogs by the dozens."

"It's evident that you like Broken Hill," commented Bony.

"No place better. I've done well."

Wally Sloan was free, in the company of a man he liked, and the 'sir' was therefore absent. A funny little man, Bony thought, and yet in his way a great man.

"You never married?" Bony asked, and the question brought a dry chuckle.

"No. Think I oughta be?"

"You're not old and beefy like those others, Sloan. You're safe enough, I think."

"You getting any warmer?" asked Sloan.

"I'm not saying. Your Mrs. Wallace said that the woman sitting next to her was got up to look half her age, and she walked upright. She was not the woman thought to have been the customer in Goldspink's shop when he was poisoned, but she carried the same hand-bag. It is Mrs. Wallace's opinion, and I am strongly inclined to rely on the opinion of a woman like Mrs. Wallace, that the woman who sat next to her was a spinster, and yet in her handbag was a baby's dummy, or comforter. What do you think about that?"

Sloan refrained from answering so long that eventually Bony looked directly at him.

"I don't know," Sloan said. "I don't understand women, and I've never met a man who did. When the Lord banished Adam and Eve from Eden, He put a gulf between men and women that's never been bridged and never will be. I know this, though, that liquor makes men and women more human, makes 'em drop their guard. And I know this, too, that there are men and women who never drink because they're afraid of other people seeing just what they are in heart and mind. That party sitting next to Mrs. Wallace drank ginger ale that afternoon because she wanted all her wits about her to poison old Gromberg, not because she never drank anything stronger. The baby's dummy stumps me."

Sloan stared down at Argent Street, and then he said:

"If Mrs. Wallace said the party was a spinster, then she was. I've known Mrs. Wallace—let me think—perhaps eleven or twelve years. She worked in the bar with me, in other pubs, too, and when you work in bars for that long you get to know men and women from the feet up. I've nothing against a man, or a woman, who doesn't drink, but I never trust anyone who doesn't drink, or smoke, or swear, or lose the old temper. Perhaps the woman with the dummy in her handbag keeps it to pretend she has a baby, and the thought of what she missed is driving her to murder."

"Perhaps that's how it is," Bony said, standing up.

"We'll go down to Argent Street for a cup of tea, and then I'll see what's turned up at the office."

They found a café open for business, and eventually parted in the street, Bony walking to Headquarters and finding it wearing its Sunday aspect. The public offices were closed, and he entered by a side door. The interior was quiet, but men were working—tough, pan-faced men with hard eyes.

Crome reported that Abbot had located a lounge habitué who remembered the woman with the blue handbag. The description given by this woman tallied with that detailed by Mrs. Wallace to Bony.

Inspector Hobson reported that he had carpeted the uniformed policeman who had been on duty near the Western Mail Hotel the previous afternoon and had been called by the head barman. This man had not seen the woman carrying the handbag which had been imprinted on his mind by Bony's pictures.

There was a conference in Bony's office that night, Hobson and Pavier, Crome and Abbot being present. There was no formality. The night was hot and Crome and Hobson discarded their coats, and everyone smoked. Suggestions were offered, thrashed out, discarded.

Pavier voiced what Crome and Abbot were thinking:

"We might get somewhere if we knew all that's in Bonaparte's mind."

"You would find only confusion," Bony told them. "I can see nothing clearly. We can be confident that a woman is responsible for these cyanidings. The progress made regarding the woman in Goldspink's shop has been nullified by the description of the woman suspected of having poisoned Gromberg's beer. The handbag is the only common link. The woman who poisoned Goldspink's tea isn't the same as she who poisoned Gromberg—unless she is a master of disguise.

"There is another point. I cannot say with any degree of confidence that the poisoner selects her victims after a study of them based on acquaintance, or that she merely carries the poison wherever she goes and drops a pinch in a drink to be taken by a victim met by chance. I am not going to put forward a theory which isn't founded on reasonable assumption. I have in mind several theories, one of which may produce an important lead, but as yet they are too nebulous to call for united action.

"As you know, in another office Artist Mills is working to give us pictures of the woman in the hotel lounge, Mrs. Wallace and that woman interviewed by Abbot being with him to direct his efforts. In the morning we'll have every man look at those new pictures before going on duty, and we'll compare the two sets for something in common to give a distinctive feature.

"I suggest that Abbot be placed in charge of what we'll call the Gallery. We'll have the two sets of pictures displayed and all those people who came in contact with the originals taken to the Gallery, and so cross-check. Something may come from that, and meanwhile every man must be doubly alerted to look for any woman bearing any resemblance to the woman in either set of pictures."

It was after ten o'clock when word came that Mills had completed his pictures, and they trooped along to the general Detective Office to see them. Mrs. Wallace enthusiastically claimed that they were 'pretty good', and the second woman said that the dress and the hat and handbag were almost exact.

The women and Mills were thanked by Superintendent Pavier, urged to remain silent, and sent home in a police car. Pavier and Hobson and Crome then went home, leaving Abbot, who was the officer on duty that night, and Bony, who wandered back to his office. He had been there less than half an hour when a constable appeared, to say that Luke Pavier wanted to see him.

Bony assented. He was feeling tired and balked, and yet tensed because the greater the difficulties, the more did an investigation captivate him. Although he had pictured Time as a Thing compressing death between forefinger and thumb, Time had other guises much less horrific, and one was the Revealer of Secrets.

Luke came in, youthful and cheerful, a tonic. Without invitation he drew a chair to the desk and sat down.

"Evening, Mr. Friend. How's the mighty brain?"

"Ageing, Luke."

"Needing a squirt of optimism, eh? Thought so. The old man's not too cheerful these days, and he's a good barometer. Nothing come out of that conference of top-graders?"

"Conference, Luke?"

"That's what I said. When the top-graders emerge all together to go home, they've been talking. When they bid each other good night as though they're suffering from indigestion, the conference was abortive. Deductive reasoning, my dear Mr. Friend."

"You should have been a detective," Bony said pleasantly.

"Not as interesting as my game. By the way, remember my Mr. Makepiece, the butcher? Surprised that Gromberg copped it and not he. Weren't you?"

"No. Your friend lacks one essential for a murderee."

"What's that?"

"He's too fastidious in eating and drinking. What are you putting into your paper to-morrow?"

" 'We regret to announce the death by cyanide poisoning of Mr. Hans Gromberg, the noted metallurgist. The late gent was born in Kiel, Germany, and came to Australia at the age of twenty-one. He was well known for his work among sick children during the twenty-three years he resided in Broken Hill. A bachelor, Mr. Gromberg was fifty-nine years old and liked his mushrooms and his beer. We understand that the police are making inquiries.' Now when are you going to let me see those drawings done by friend Mills?"

"Drawings, Luke? 'Oh, Grandmamma, what long ears you have!' "

" 'Oh, Grandmamma, what sharp teeth you have,' the little lady in red also exclaimed. What about those pictures? When are you going to decide that I may be able to help you along?"

"When I've decided that I can trust you."

"You can begin now, Mr. Friend. These cyanidings have passed beyond a joke between the old man and Crome on the one side and me on the other. Deep under, I've got a lot of time for the old man. He's nearing the retiring age, and it might be that he'll retire with his reputation all smeared over by Stillman and other rats. I can't afford to be the son of a man with a ruined reputation."

The sophistication was so obviously spurious that Bony wanted to smile.

"Let us make a pact," he said. "You to print only what I agree to. I to accept your co-operation and avail myself of your experience and knowledge of local conditions. And you to be present at the arrest and then be free to publish what you wish."

"I'll sign."

"Come with me."

Luke followed Bony to the detectives' common-room, a place of desks and records and pictures of criminals. On one wall were the five water-colours done by David Mills. Bony sat on a desk, and Luke went forward to study the pictures. He was there for what appeared to be a long time, and on rejoining Bony he said:

"Somewhere, sometime, I've seen the woman in the blue and white dress and the white hat."

"The face or the dress?"

"Face."

"Remember ever having seen the handbag?"

Pavier went back to the pictures and returned, shaking his head.

"The face is like someone I know, but I can't place her. I will. What's her name?"

"She hasn't a name. Mills painted her from a description given him by two women who were in the lounge when Gromberg died. The three other pictures were done by Mills from the very few details given by Mary Isaacs of the customer she was serving when Goldspink died."

"Those three don't help. Same handbag, though?"

"Same handbag. Come back to the office." When

behind his desk, Bony said: "If you can recall anyone who looks like Mills's women, let me know. Mills told me, or rather his girl friend did, that he has appeared at local concerts as a lightning cartoonist. Perhaps the women you are trying to remember has engaged in amateur theatricals. Come in and look at those pictures when you wish. I'll see to it that you'll have no difficulty."

"Thanks. What d'you think? Woman on border line of insanity?"

"As the motive for these murders is not to be found among those prompting ninety-nine murders in every hundred, yes. Ever read *Macbeth* or seen the play?"

"Both. I'm interested in the theatre. Have you read Professor J. I. M. Stewart's book, *Character and Motive in Shakespeare*?"

"No," admitted Bony.

"The professor says, and I quote: 'The evil which may rise up in a man's imagination may sweep him on to crime, particularly if, like Macbeth, he is imaginative without the release of being creative.'"

"That," Bony said, "is the word picture of the woman I seek. Thank you, Luke. I seek a motive within a motive, however. I am sure that the motive prompting these poisonings is hatred of someone each victim represents, not hatred of the victims. It is a chain of cause and effect, the ultimate effect being the death of men having nothing whatsoever to do with the original cause."

The quiet building appeared to come to life, and on Bony's ceasing to speak, Luke dried up. It was after eleven at night on that one day of the week when Headquarters permitted itself to doze, and now men were tramping corridors with decided urgency in their footsteps.

"Something doing," Luke said very softly, and the muscular tautness was evident.

From the rear of the building came the crash of a motor engine and, following the initial power surge, its quiet purring. They could follow the sound of the machine making for the street.

"Fire, perhaps," murmured Bony, watching Luke.

"Perhaps another killing," said Luke. "Sounds promisin', anyway. See you some more, Mr. Friend."

He vanished beyond the open doorway, and his steps could be heard as he ran along the corridors to the public offices and the constable on night duty at the telephone switch. Bony waited five minutes before engaging Switch.

"Inspector Bonaparte. What's the hullabaloo about?"

"Don't rightly know, sir," came the reply. "A mineworker returning home on account of sickness tripped over the body of a woman at the foot of a mullock dump. He reported the matter to a patrol officer, who telephoned here. I put him through to Senior Detective Abbot, who's on night duty, sir."

Bony hung up, hoping it was not another cyaniding, and proceeding to note lines of thought emerging from the conference earlier in the evening.

It was after one o'clock when he put down his pen and locked away his papers, and he was rolling a cigarette when he heard the corridors again resounding with heavy feet. Crome burst in on him, his face windwhipped, his hair all awry.

"Guess who we've got in the morgue with old Gromberg!" he said.

"I'm a poor guesser," Bony told him.

"None other than our own dear Policewoman Lodding."

CHAPTER THIRTEEN

Feminine Observations

A man on maintenance work at one of the mines had reported sick and, having checked out with the time-keeper, he had made his way down through the top hamper of the mine to reach a path crossing the sandy and littered flat to one of the abutting streets. It was quite dark, but, being familiar with the path, he was able to follow it, and where it skirted a mullock dump he almost tripped over the body. He had ascertained, with the aid of a match, that the body was that of a woman and, being a member of a First Aid Section, he recognised death.

Crome, who lived farthest from Headquarters, had been eating supper when recalled. He arrived at the scene with a doctor a few minutes after Abbot, who had collected several men. The doctor found the blade of a knife buried in the woman's breast, and the place was cordoned and the body brought to the city morgue.

Bony, having met Policewoman Lodding, was shocked but determined not to be sidetracked from his own investigation. Crome was confident that he could deal with this type of homicide and raised for discussion the division of forces. It was agreed that Bony retain as his assistants Senior Detective Abbot and another man, and so by daybreak Crome had ample forces, which included black trackers, and Bony and Abbot were in bed.

Later Abbot was first at Headquarters, Bony being delayed by an interview with Mrs. Robinov.

"You have a car?" he asked Abbot, who said he owned a motor-cycle. "Hopeless to ask for a police car, and I want you to call on Mrs. Wallace and that Mrs. Lucas you saw yesterday and persuade them to come to Goldspink's shop at two this afternoon. Explain to them that their advice and assistance is needed with reference to the pictures they saw Mills paint last night."

"Very well, sir."

"How is that other affair ccoming along?"

"Don't know much about it," replied Abbot. "Sergeant Crome is still out. I did hear that the knife blade in Miss Lodding's body is made of glass. Where the blade joins the hilt a file was used to make a circular cut, so weakening the weapon that after the blow was delivered the murderer was able to snap off the hilt, leaving the blade in the wound and preventing bleeding."

"A glass dagger, Abbot! Peculiar kind of weapon."

"That's so, sir. Light blue glass, triangular down to an inch of the point."

"Well, don't let us be diverted from our own job," Bony said. "Our three murders are quite enough to keep us fully extended."

Abbot left, and Bony telephoned David Mills and arranged that Mills also be at Goldspink's shop at two o'clock, taking his painting materials. At eleven Luke Pavier rang.

"This Lodding business, Mr. Friend," Luke said. "It doesn't come into our agreement, does it?"

"No, Luke, you can go your hardest."

"Anything for me," pleaded the reporter, "on this Lodding murder?"

"Nothing. I know nothing. Haven't seen Crome this morning."

"All right. We're putting out a special. I found a laddie and his lass who saw the Lodding woman in the company of a man late last night. Just beat Crome to it. Reduced the stuff about Gromberg to five lines. That please you?"

"It does."

"These women," Luke ran on. "The straight-backed, flat-chested Lodding walking out with a man. What d'ya think? Passed under a street light. Man's arm linked through hers. Tall and handsome gentleman who wore gloves. Bad luck the lovers didn't see his face. Old Crome shouldn't fall down on this job, though. See you later."

Crome didn't think he would, either. He dropped in on Bony to relate his progress, describing how the trackers had back-tracked the murdered woman and her companion to a street ending abruptly at the narrow flat of waste ground. It was in that street they had been seen by the lovers, who stood just inside a garden gate.

"Trackers are now looking for the handle of the dagger," Crome said. "I made good plaster casts of the man's tracks. Like to see 'em sometime?"

"Yes, sometime. Should find Miss Lodding's companion easily enough. The number of her male acquaintances was not large, I understand."

"That's so. I'm off to question the sister. A Mrs. Dalton. Bit rough on you, however."

Bony reflected. He wanted to be generous to Crome, who now had the opportunity to regain lost prestige.

"Don't worry about my end. Concentrate on your job. For several reasons I hope you clean it up quickly."

Crome was pleased and left. Almost immediately Superintendent Pavier rang through.

"Any developments, Bonaparte?"

"Nothing, Super. But——"

"That's all right. I'm going with Crome to visit Miss Lodding's sister and dig into backgrounds. We must show Sydney this time."

The Detective Office was vacant except for the man assigned to Bony under Abbot. He was asked to remove the paintings from the wall, and as he had been typing rather speedily, Bony asked if he could write shorthand. The detective said he could, and, having accepted the parcelled pictures, Bony told him to be at Goldspink's shop at two o'clock.

At two, to the minute, Bony entered the shop and was met by Mrs. Robinov.

"Everyone's in the fitting-room, Inspector."

He smiled his approval of such punctuality, and she conducted him to the fitting-room, where waited Mrs. Wallace and Mrs. Lucas, Mary Isaacs, Miss Way, Abbot with his assistant, and David Mills.

Bony thanked them for being present, and they were made to feel 'awfully important'. He had the plain-clothes man tack the pictures to a wall and then arranged the gathering as though children seated before a blackboard. Mills was placed at the cutting table and asked to prepare his materials.

"It is important that you are silent concerning this little session," Bony began, "because I want to take you into my confidence and be able to discuss with you freely certain grave difficulties confronting me in unearthing this vile poisoner.

"Now look at these pictures so ably painted by Mr. Mills. These three to the left represent the woman who was present shortly before Mr. Goldspink died, and these two on the right represent the woman present in the hotel lounge to within a few minutes of the death of Mr. Gromberg.

"We know that neither Mrs. Robinov, Miss Isaacs, nor Miss Way can see in the picture of the lounge woman the woman they saw in the shop, and although two women could have carried the same handbag, the circumstances are such as to make us certain that one woman committed both crimes.

"This woman is clever. She isn't a novice. She doesn't make mistakes, and she did not make the great mistake of adopting a disguise after committing a crime, but before she committed it.

"At once divest your minds of the picture of a woman wearing a false wig and dark glasses and the uniform of a nurse or something of the kind. When she came here to the shop she seemed to be elderly, she had a stoop, and she used her eyes as though by habit peering over glasses. That is the impression she gave Miss Isaacs and, in lesser degree, Miss Way. When she went to the hotel lounge she appeared very much younger, did not peer as though over glasses, didn't have a stoop, and wore clothes suitable for a woman of, say, thirty. With reason, therefore, we may assess her real age at from forty to forty-five.

"There is the remote possibility that the person seen by you ladies is a man disguised as a woman. We must take into account that there have been and are extremely clever female impersonators both on the stage and off, and before we proceed let us settle that point. You, Mrs. Wallace, do you think that the person who sat next you on Saturday afternoon could have been a man disguised as a woman?"

Mrs. Wallace was most indignant. "Not a hope. I know *all* the differences between a man and a woman."

"What makes you so certain?" questioned the unabashed Bony.

"Because I'd soon smell the difference," claimed Mrs. Wallace, and Bony hastily changed the subject.

"We then reject the possibility that the person was a man disguised as a woman. Did the woman betray any evidence to you, Mrs. Wallace, that she was shortsighted?"

"I'm sure there wasn't anything wrong with her eyesight. I remember telling you that she fumbled with her purse, but that wasn't shortsightedness. It musta been because she was all steamed up to skittle old Gromberg, though I still say I never saw her do anything to his beer."

"Then let us discuss the woman's face. Her make-up, you say, was heavily applied. How near did Mr. Mills paint the faces to what you remember of the woman's make-up?"

"Pretty close, but not quite, Inspector." Mrs. Wallace

became triumphant. "I remember the lipstick she had on."

"She had on the wrong lipstick," interposed Mrs. Lucas.

"She did that," Mrs. Wallace agreed. "It didn't give her anything."

"Looked to me as if she was an amateur at putting her face on," said Mrs. Lucas, and again Mrs. Wallace agreed.

"An amateur—or it could have been done purposely to achieve an amateurish effect," Bony pointed out. "You said, Mrs. Wallace, didn't you, that the woman looked like an old maid who had ventured into——"

"Hell or a harem," added Mrs. Wallace. "If she wasn't an old maid she acted pretty well, is what I say and what I think. I can tell 'em in spite of all their titivating."

"How did she appear to you, Mrs. Lucas?"

"I didn't take that much notice, Inspector, but I've a sort of impression that Mrs. Wallace is right."

"Thank you. Well, now, because you two ladies remember that woman so clearly, and Miss Isaacs and Miss Way do not clearly remember the woman who visited the shop, we will discard these three pictures of her as and when she was served by Miss Isaacs." He took the three paintings from the wall. "We have now only the two pictures of the woman seen in the lounge. Mrs. Wallace, which of these two pictures is nearer your memory of the woman?"

"That one on the right, although the dress on her isn't as good as in the other picture."

"We will leave the dress for the moment. Mrs. Lucas, which is your choice of pictures?"

"That one Mrs. Wallace picked."

"Good. We will now discard the left one," and Bony removed it. "Now, Mr. Mills, will you try to draw this woman's head without make-up, and to your notion of what she would be like, say, at forty-five."

David Mills took fifteen minutes. Bony produced cigarettes, and Abbot's assistant rounded off his notes. Mrs. Wallace began to discuss the suspect's clothes and was asked to refrain. She was the first to be shown the new face.

"Pretty good," was her verdict, "but the chin isn't square enough, and the eyes ought to be a bit slanted down at the outside corners."

"I'll make the alterations easily enough," volunteered Mills.

He took the draft sketch, and Mrs. Wallace went to stand by him, saying:

"When you've done that, I'll tell you just where to put in the wrinkles. Her make-up didn't hide them from me." Using an eraser, Mills swiftly went to work. "That's good for the mouth. Yes, and good for the eyes too. Come and have a look, dearie."

Mrs. Lucas was drawn into conference, and both agreed that the result was 'just it'.

"You're a beaut, Mr. Mills," exclaimed the ex-barmaid. "You've got the livin' image, hasn't he, Mrs. Lucas?"

Mrs. Lucas agreed again with Mrs. Wallace, and Bony handed the black and white drawing to Mrs. Robinov, who said she didn't know a woman like her. Mary Isaacs hesitated long enough for Bony to say:

"Don't hurry."

Finally Mary admitted defeat, and the cashier shook her head.

"We've done very well so far," Bony said. "Now let us examine the pictured dress. How near are we at this stage, Mrs. Wallace and Mrs. Lucas?"

They both said that the dress was almost as they remembered it. It was light blue scattered with white blossoms, elbow-length sleeves and a full skirt.

"Did you notice the material?" asked Mrs. Robinov.

" 'Course I did," countered Mrs. Wallace. "I said she took it out of lavender. It was extra-heavy silk, the sort of stuff you haven't been able to buy for about fifteen years."

Mary exclaimed:

"Oh, Mrs. Robinov! You remember——"

"I'll fetch it—my wedding dress. I had it made in Harbin in 1926. It might be the same quality."

Abbot looked alarmed. Bony remained placidly patient. Mrs. Robinov hurried away, and the women questioned Mary Isaacs, their excitement making even Bony wonder. The dress was brought, displayed on the cutting table. It was off white, but the material had captured the heady sheen of the water lily.

"That's it—let me touch it," Mrs. Wallace cried. "Oh, it's gorgeous! Oh, how lovely, Mrs. Robinov."

"You say that you bought the material in Harbin," Bony inserted.

"Yes. I've never seen such silk in Australia, Inspector."

"There never was such material in Australia," Mrs. Wallace said with conviction. "If there'd been I'd have got some."

Mrs. Robinov tenderly folded the wedding frock in

the mass of tissue paper and carried it away.

"It would seem, Mrs. Wallace, that the woman in the blue silk frock at one time travelled beyond Australia," Bony said suggestively.

"Don't follow she did, Inspector. But someone who's done a bit of travellin' around has certainly brought back that material. All the best comes to the Hill, and that sort of stuff would have come, too, if it was imported."

"And we can say that Mr. Mills's pictured dress is near the reality?"

She and Mrs. Lucas agreed that it was.

"Can we say the same of the handbag?"

Mary Isaacs led the chorus of approval.

"Thank you so much, ladies. You have all been extremely helpful. I'll now run through the items which make up this woman's description as seen in the hotel lounge. Age somewhere about forty-five. Height five feet ten or eleven inches. Walks without a stoop. Shape of face more square than oval. Eyes grey. Nose straight and slightly thick. Mouth wide and lips straight. And lastly, the hair. Your description of the hair, given to Mr. Mills last night, is 'hennaed'. Will you please explain that word?"

Mrs. Lucas, who was thinking she had taken second place to Mrs. Wallace, got in first.

"Henna is used to brighten the hair and make it look like red hair. But the woman's hair wasn't properly red. Just tinted."

"Otherwise, dyed to appear what it isn't?" questioned Bony, and Mrs. Wallace giggled.

"Two out of every three women do something like

that to their hair," she said, and looked almost affectionately at Mrs. Robinov, who brought in afternoon tea. She called Mrs. Robinov 'luv' and 'dearie' and thoroughly enjoyed herself. And Bony, well pleased, walked with Abbot back to Headquarters.

"Seems that we've got something at last," Abbot said. "We should be able to find that woman now."

"Should!" echoed Bony. "We shall!"

CHAPTER FOURTEEN

Honours to Nimmo and Abbot

Jimmy Nimmo sat in a saloon bar and was unhappy. Superficially there was nothing to cause him unhappiness, for he had plenty of money, clothes which satisfied him, and proximity to a plentiful supply of cooling beer. It was the threat of hidden forces and not material things which fretted him.

He ought to be in this pleasant saloon bar reading a paper and enjoying the best cigarettes with long 'butchers' of beer. Outside was Argent Street and, if not now, then very soon there would be gimlet-eyed men walking up and down Argent Street who would recognise him, and one of them might be his arch-enemy, Inspector Stillman.

And this at the time when he was becoming increasingly interested in the stone-built two-storeyed house offering so much promise. The third poisoning would be bound to stir up the entire police force and interfere with the routine of the night patrols with which he had made himself familiar.

Jimmy hadn't to be told the police set-up. He knew that Bonaparte was a Queenslander—seconded to New South Wales to investigate a series of poisoning cases— and he knew also that the Queenslander would not be permitted to undertake in addition the case of Police-woman Lodding. She had been a member of the Police Department, and nothing stirs up a police department more than the killing of one of its own. Therefore, if Crome and his boys failed to ring the bell, the Sydney mob would barge in, pronto.

Following four murders, Broken Hill was no place for a respectable burglar.

Jimmy wanted to leave 'toot sweet', and this he dared not do without Bonaparte's permission. It was just too bad, for there were two strong attractions for him in Broken Hill: one, that two-storeyed house, and the other for whose sake he might even retire from his profession. The major problem was that the lady for whom he yearned expected him to take her to cinemas and other places of amusement and would wonder why he kept to his room by day as well as by night.

It was Tuesday, too, and the policewoman was found late on the Sunday night. The bar clock said fourteen minutes past eleven, and any action was better than being a sitting shot.

Jimmy went out and found a telephone.

"Mornin', Inspector! How's things?" he asked Bony.

"Tip-top, Jimmy. And how are you?"

"Pining to associate with the ruddy police. What about a chin-wag?"

"Certainly. Have lunch with me. See you at the Western Mail at one."

Jimmy returned to the saloon bar and ordered more beer. For the tenth time he read the latest on the Lodding murder. There was something he might use to wangle permission to leave Broken Hill by the Adelaide

Express that evening. At five past one he was seated at a table with Inspector Bonaparte.

"Been getting around?" inquired Bony.

"Yes and no. You been busy?"

"Very. Not able to relax like you, you know."

Jimmy tried to see behind the bland blue eyes, failed, and set to work on the fish. Bony was kind.

"I've brought a picture to show you before we leave. Tell me, since being here have you noticed many elderly men with food-stained shirt fronts?"

"One—or two. You meet 'em in pubs sometimes. Any reason?"

"Only that the three poisoned men were like those I've described."

Jimmy declined to look into the blue eyes and feigned interest in the cut from the sirloin.

"Had a letter from an aunt down in Adelaide," he said. "Pretty sick. Plenty of dough. Wants me to run down and visit her."

"She will doubtless recover."

"Then make a new will leaving me out of it—if I don't kiss her on the sick-bed."

"What part of her would that be?"

Jimmy scorned Bony's question, saying:

"Met a man who was elderly, well set-up, fairly well dressed. Food spots on the front of his double-breaster. The paper reminds me of him."

"Good of you to get away from the sick aunt. Mustard?"

"No, thanks. Leave me to a chunk of think."

They were eating the sweet when Bony remarked:

"You mentioned a chunk of think, Jimmy."

"Yes, so I did. You still guarantee I'm not pinched if I walk up and down Argent Street with me chest thrown out like a real big man?"

"There's no need to question that—or to discuss it. Let's have that chunk of think in connection with something you've read in the newspaper."

"Well, it pans out like this—and I'm relying on your guarantee." Jimmy waited for additional assurance and, not receiving it, resignedly continued. "Yesterday and to-day the papers say that the spooning pair who saw the Lodding wench on Sunday night say they think that the man she was with was tall and smartly dressed. They saw him and Lodding as they passed beneath a street light, but where they were standing was too far from the light to see clothes colours.

"The girl with her Romeo says she recognised Lodding but not the man. He was wearing a felt which shadowed his face. His arm was linked through Lodding's, and they looked real matey-like. And they say the fella was wearing gloves—dark gloves. That right?"

"All that is correct, Jimmy."

"About a week ago I was out for a stroll in the cool of the evening," proceeded Jimmy, and did not add that he was strolling about the locality of the two-storeyed house. "Passing one of those corner eateries, I saw a man I'd met once before: big fella, well rigged, carrying black gloves. I recognised him by his strut and by his dark grey mo. The first time I saw him he had a goatee to match. I take a good eyeful of anything I meet in the streets and I haven't seen anyone else sporting gloves in Broken Hill."

The coffee was served, and Bony rolled and lit a cigarette before he prompted:

"You saw this man prior to this meeting?"

"I did. I saw him buying black leather gloves at Goldspink's shop, and I'm pretty sure that the gloves he carried that night were the same gloves. But that night he didn't have a beard. He had a different suit on too. When I saw him in Goldspink's he was wearing a grey double-breaster. It was a swank suit and fairly new. I remember thinking that the dirty blighter oughta have it cleaned."

Bony jotted the notes on the back of a menu card and gained further items concerning the man who had bought gloves. The man's eyebrows and moustache and beard were closely described by one self-trained in the difficult 'art' of observation. Jimmy mimicked the voice, and, when again in the street, Bony said:

"Thanks, Jimmy. Keep in mind that you'll be a gone coon if you leave Broken Hill without my knowledge. Don't permit thought of the boys from Sydney to upset the gastric juices after that pleasant lunch. You are working for me, and no one will break your employment. Get around. You know where I am if you spot that man again, or a woman like the picture I've shown you."

Now feeling much better, and free to concentrate on the two-storeyed house and the lady he referred to as 'the attraction', Jimmy decided on a game or two of billiards, and Bony pensively sauntered back to Headquarters.

Crome was not in his office, and he rang for Abbot. "The sergeant and several of the men are in conference with Superintendent Pavier, sir."

Their gaze clashed, and both men understood that conference more often than not is spelled c-h-e-c-k-m-a-t-e.

"You can manage a typewriter, I suppose?" Bony said.

"Yes, sir."

"Type this description in triplicate, and let me have it when done. Don't let anyone else see it. Oh, and have this head of our woman nailed to the wall beside the other pictures. See to it that every uniformed man studies it."

Abbot departed. Bony rolled six cigarettes, lit the first, and pushed back his chair that he might rest his feet on the desk. He sought for and failed to find any connection between the murder of a policewoman and the murder of three elderly bachelors—save food-spotted clothes. The butts of four of the six cigarettes had been added to those in the saucer ash-tray when Abbot returned.

"The three copies of the man," he said, placing the typed sheets before Bony. His expression was normal, but the manner in which he finger-combed his fair hair betrayed excitement. "The man's description struck a chord, sir, and I went into Records. Brought out George Henry Tuttaway."

Abbot presented two official pictures of a man who had not voluntarily posed for them. He was big-boned, handsome, clean-shaven, and at the foot of each picture was the name 'George Henry Tuttaway'. Abbot presented a card, and Bony read:

"Tuttaway, George Henry: Indicted Melbourne 1940 for abduction and illegal confinement. Sentenced to be held during Governor's pleasure. Escaped from Ballarat Gaol 27 September 1949. Professional magician internationally known as the Great Scarsby. Conduct in gaol good, but thought could be dangerous. Declared mentally abnormal." There was appended a description which roughly tallied with the man seen twice by Jimmy Nimmo.

"Crome should be happy," Bony said, but Abbot wanted confirmation.

"Think your man is Tuttaway, sir?"

"More than possible. My man was seen in Goldspink's shop buying black kid gloves. He was seen subsequently by the same person one night and was then carrying the gloves. The Great Scarsby. I can't recall the name. Must have been in the interior when he was sentenced. You know anything of him?"

"Not much, sir. Don't remember if he came to Australia as the Great Scarsby. Remember, of course, seeing the report of the escape when it came in."

"A magician!" murmured Bony. "Quick-change artist, and that kind of thing. Wonder if, in spite of what those women said, our poisoner is a man got up as a woman. Declared mentally abnormal. Ah, conference ended."

The pictures and the card dealing with Tuttaway, Bony slipped under the blotter. Men were approaching along the corridor. They heard Crome go into his office. The second man came on, entered. It was Pavier. Without invitation he sat down and lit a cigarette.

"How are you getting on?"

"Slowly, Super, slowly," replied Bony, and Abbot went out. "How is Crome?"

"Stopped. What are your impressions of my late secretary?"

"Efficient. Humourless."

"I found her so, and very reticent. Never attempted to probe into her private life. Instinctively felt that she was highly moral and not interested in men. The married sister—a Mrs. Dalton—says she had neither men nor women friends. The girl standing inside the gate with her sweetheart says she worked with Muriel Lodding for some time—for a firm of stock and station agents—and even then Lodding exhibited no interest in men. We can't trace any contact between the murdered woman and a man, and yet she was seen on Sunday night walking arm in arm with one. And, Bonaparte, those two lovers can't give us anything like a clear description of him. I feel strongly urged to call on Sydney for assistance."

"Tell me, why did you come to see me and not send for me?"

"Because I don't want to do what I feel I must do. Will you give Crome a hand? I know it isn't fair to ask, but you might find a lead for us to follow. What Crome wants is one per cent of your confidence. It's what I need too. The confidence we did have has been bashed to pulp."

"I'll call Crome," Bony decided, and, leaning back, thumped the partition wall. Crome came in, stood stiffly erect.

"Sit down, Bill," Bony invited, and the sergeant blinked. To Pavier, Bony said:

"You always inspect incoming and outgoing trains and aircraft, but you have ignored road traffic. Think you could have every truck and car leaving Broken Hill inspected?"

The Superintendent said they could.

"It might be too late, but I think not," Bony proceeded, and took up Abbot's typescript. "The man you want answers to this description."

Presenting each with a copy, he leaned back and watched them. Then one man followed the other in looking up at him, expectantly, hopefully.

"That is the description of the man who might be able to tell you something about the murder of Muriel Lodding," Bony said. "Fortunately for us, and the public, the great majority of murders spring from common causes such as jealousy, greed, frustration. Murder actuated by passion, the unpremeditated murder, is easy to finalise and never worthy of my attention.

"Murder, however, which has its genesis in the mind bordering on insanity presents a much greater problem to the investigator because the two minds don't motivate alike. The only major weapon to be used by a sane investigator in his battle with a near-insane killer is, my dear Pavier, patience. The patience of the tiger cat—of Death—of Inspector Napoleon Bonaparte."

Pavier would have spoken had not Crome cleared his throat.

"If you apprehend a man answering to that description," Bony said, "I feel sure he will be the man you want for the murder of Muriel Lodding. Further, due to Abbot's astuteness, I am strongly of the opinion that his name is George Henry Tuttaway, known on the other side of the world as the Great Scarsby."

Detective Sergeant Crome forgot the Superintendent. He leaned over the desk and, eyes flashing, exclaimed:

"Well, I'll be damned!"

CHAPTER FIFTEEN

Assist and Be Assisted

With Crome, Bony went over the scene of the Lodding murder. He was shown the light standard beside which Muriel Lodding and her escort had been seen by the lovers and the gateway inside which they had stood. He was taken to the end of the street, which terminated at the belt of waste ground extending to the large mullock dump at the foot of the broken hill.

The story told by the aboriginal trackers had to be reconstructed, for they had begun at the middle and had to work backwards and then forwards to its completion.

The end of the paved street was fifty-seven yards beyond the last of the houses, and near where one stepped from the made road to the sandy waste was the scene of the killing. It was here that the story told by the trackers actually began.

When the man stepped off the hard pavement he was carrying the woman. Behind him the nearest street light, that under which he had been seen with his victim, was approximately two hundred yards distant. Before him was the blacked-out sand waste, beyond which the superstructure of the mines stood sharply revealed by floodlights. Against the foot of the broken hill and grey mullock dump could not be seen at night.

The murderer had carried his victim for nine hundred-odd yards before that mullock dump loomed ahead of him, and then he had dropped the body and stood hesitant about his next move. That had been to trudge back across the sand waste towards the distinctive lighting of Argent Street.

It was Crome's theory that the story told by the trackers indicated that the murderer was a stranger to Broken Hill, for every man working at the mine beyond the dump would know that path tramped hard by their feet and used daily by dozens who rode a bicycle to and from work. Having arrived at the end of the street, the man had killed his victim, intending to dispose of the body among the mine machinery and thus divert suspicion in the mind of anyone who had chanced to see him with the woman. Faced by the steep wall of the mullock dump, he had not seen the path and, wearied by the trek across the sand, he decided finally to drop the body there.

This theory was supported, as to the stranger in Broken Hill, by the fact that no miner would be unaware of what aborigines can read on impressionable surfaces, and no other resident of Broken Hill would be ignorant of it, either. In all of this Bony concurred, and Crome's confidence rose a fraction of the percentage Pavier said was needful.

Again at Headquarters, Bony was shown the knife blade. It was seven inches in length, fluted in triangular shape to within an inch of the fine point. That it had been partly filed through close to the haft was evident, and the purpose had been effectual because the wound had not bled. After that came the plaster casts of the murderer's footprints made by shoes size eight, worn slightly at the back of the heels and at no particular edge of the soles.

"Certainly a large man and heavy," Bony said. "He struts in the manner of the egotist, head up, shoulders squared. It'll be Tuttaway without doubt. Telegraph Melbourne for all available information concerning the history of the man, as well as the medical history, and ask if the gaol authorities have a boot or shoe worn by Tuttaway. Urge prompt despatch by air, Crome, for I cannot spend too much time on this case."

"I'll do it at once—and thank you, sir."

Left alone, Bony perused the transcript of notes taken by Crome of Pavier's interview with the dead woman's sister. It was quickly seen that the conversation was confined to the immediate past, for Pavier would have known, and the Staff Records would include, the details of Policewoman Lodding's previous employment and places of abode.

It could be accepted with certainty that the murdered woman knew her companion of that night, for she was as remote from the pick-up type as platinum is from lead. And yet her sister had declared repeatedly to Pavier that Muriel Lodding had no male friends with whom she was sufficiently intimate to walk arm in arm at night. The two women lived quietly. Both disliked the cinema but often went to a concert or a lecture. Their interests were identical, and men were not included.

Bony rang Pavier.

"What were your impressions of Mrs. Dalton?" he asked.

"Quite good," replied Pavier. "Slightly older than Lodding but still attractive. Was positive that her sister hadn't a man friend in Broken Hill. I pressed the matter further, went back to the years before they came here, and Mrs. Dalton was equally emphatic that Lodding had never shown interest in any man. Used to tax her about it, warn her she'd become a sour old maid."

"So I see from the transcript, sir. Extraordinary set-up."

Bony read the statements obtained from the sweethearts. Time and circumstances and identification of the man as far as it went were identical in both statements. That made by the girl gave more, but not much more than the records would provide.

Staff Records did not help much.

Muriel Lodding and her sister arrived in Australia from London in June 1936. They had lived in Sydney from that date until transferring to Broken Hill in November 1938. In Sydney the dead woman worked for a firm of wool brokers and station agents, and the transfer to Broken Hill had been dictated by the Broken Hill office of the same firm. She had remained with the Broken Hill office for two years, left to work for a solicitor, and finally joined the clerical staff of the Police Department, subsequently ranking as senior policewoman only for salary.

Next morning before eleven Crome came into Bony's office with a substantial package.

"Just arrived from Melbourne by special air freight," he announced, and proceeded to remove the covering to disclose a pair of shoes and a long official envelope.

"Those casts," snapped Bony.

Crome brought them, surprising Bony by his swiftness of movement. They were compared with the shoes, and there was triumph in the sergeant's eyes when they met the gleaming blue eyes over the laden desk.

"Tuttaway, all right," Bony stated. "I'm expecting a great friend of mine at any moment. He'll clinch it, I'm sure. Open the report."

There was a covering letter, which Crome put aside pro tem. The report was detailed, and the gist of it ran thus:

Tuttaway was born in Birmingham, England, in 1880. The son of a hardware merchant, he had been educated at Winchester and Cambridge. Became prominent in vaudeville in 1907, was associated for several years with the Great Martini, and shortly after World War I formed a company of his own which he took on tour through Europe and North and South America. He had disbanded the company in 1937, in which year he had come to Australia. The following year he bought a property at Doncaster, Victoria.

The property was valuable, the house being large and built in a previous era, and the grounds extensive. There he lived the life of a recluse, keeping no staff and no outside domestic help. First evidence of a disordered mind was when he had twenty acres of valuable fruit trees cut down for no apparent reason.

A girl aged sixteen disappeared from the nearby district of Lilydale, and eventually she was found in Tuttaway's house, where she had been confined in a cellar for five months. On being rescued, she was physically healthy and clean, but mentally prostrate. Under nursing care she was able to tell the story of her abduction and imprisonment.

Tuttaway, the once famed Great Scarsby, hammered incessantly to make her a magnificent magician, told her that he would present her to the world as such. It mattered nothing to him that the girl didn't want to be a magician. When she failed to master simple tricks and refused to practise, he caned her, twisted her arms, and sometimes forced her to stand on her toes with her thumbs noosed to the wall.

He ranted at her stubbornness and raved about her beautiful, useless hands.

When the police found the girl he threw himself at her feet and implored her to remain with him and become the greatest magician the world had ever known. The verdict was inevitable.

His behaviour in gaol was exemplary, and progress of the mental illness appeared to be arrested. Consequently he was granted a measure of freedom.

The break had been effected sometime in the afternoon of 27 September 1949. He was not missed until five-fifteen and had not since been sighted with certainty as to identification.

"It'll be him," confidently asserted Crome. "Must have come in by road."

"All the police on those road exits?"

"Too right. If he didn't clear out immediately after murdering Lodding, then the only way he can get out now is through the scrub. And he's no bushman."

"We'll see if my friend is waiting," Bony decided, and rang the public office. Mr. James Nimmo was waiting.

Jimmy appeared, escorted by a uniformed constable. To Jimmy's relief, the constable withdrew, but this was counted out by the glimmer of recognition in the small grey eyes of the large man he had taped a policeman long ago. Jimmy was elegantly attired in grey tweed with a faint red stripe.

"Glad to see you, Jimmy," Bony said smoothly. "This is Detective Sergeant Crome. Meet Mr. Nimmo, Crome."

Before the sergeant realised it, he held out his hand, saying:

"Pleased to meet you, Mr. Nimmo." Jimmy awkwardly accepted the offered fist, smiled faintly, as though faint, sat down in the indicated chair, and regarded Bony reproachfully. Nonchalantly Bony said:

"Ever seen this man, Jimmy?"

Jimmy accepted the official pictures, appeared to edge a fraction farther away from Crome, who sat beside him, and examined the pictures of George Henry Tuttaway.

"Yes, that's the fella I saw at Goldspink's," he said without looking up. "When I saw him he had a grey moustache and goatee ziff. It's easy."

"Sure?" asked Crome from force of habit.

"Like ourselves, Crome, Mr. Nimmo is a professional observer of faces," Bony cut in. "As you see at the foot of the pictures, Jimmy, the man's stage name is the Great Scarsby. Remember the case?"

"Yes, I do," answered Jimmy, memory vivid of being seated in a heavy truck and hearing two drivers discuss the escape of Tuttaway. "First time I seen his picture, though. Supposed to be batty, wasn't he?"

"Is," corrected Bony. "Well, thanks, Jimmy, for coming along. See you again sometime. Leave you to find your way out."

Jimmy got up, nodded to Crome, smiled at Bony, and vanished. Bony waited for his footsteps to die away before saying:

"Good man, that. Ought to have been a detective. Now that we are sure that your murderer is the escaped Tuttaway, I suggest we give Luke Pavier the entire story for publication to-morrow. If Tuttaway is still in Broken Hill, that will make him bolt, and one of the road patrols will nab him. If you don't sight him within three days, you can accept the fact that he cleared out before the roads were blocked."

"Fair enough, sir. Meanwhile I'll keep this set of fingerprints and other data close to hand. I've men hunting antique shops and others where the knife might have been sold to Tuttaway. By the way, I've seen your Mr. Nimmo before."

"Without doubt, Crome. My friend has been in Broken Hill for several months. On holiday, you know, but not averse to doing a small job now and then. He's a burglar, and on several occasions I have found him invaluable."

"A burg——" Sergeant Crome broke off and gave a low respectful whistle, saying: "Perhaps I can now see through a brick wall, and the recovery of that loot from three break-and-entries."

"There were no breakings, Crome. Just enterings."

The sergeant's face reddened. He almost gaped, caught himself in time, and stood stiffly to attention.

"Yes, sir," he said, almost as though he agreed.

"I may have to use Mr. Nimmo again, Crome. That

is but one of his names and not the name he uses when in Sydney. What is theft compared with homicide? My friend is an expert burglar, almost an artist. I admire experts, no matter in what field, and I never hesitate to use such talent in my search for a killer."

"But a burg——"

Crome began to laugh, checked himself, really laughed, and Bony gravely advised:

"Keep your eyes on a star, and let not your gaze be diverted by lesser illuminants. Use the lesser luminaries to light your way to reach the star. Your star is the Great Scarsby."

CHAPTER SIXTEEN

Many a Slip . . .

Two days passed, yielding nothing. Men questioned and probed: and Superintendent Pavier forgot the date terminating Bony's association with his police division: and the Great Scarsby remained elusive.

The murder of Policewoman Lodding almost overshadowed that of Hans Gromberg, owing in distinct measure to Luke Pavier, and Wally Sloan reported there was no falling off of lounge trade. The public were wholly absorbed in the hunt for the Great Scarsby.

Friday afternoon came round again, and Patrick O'Hara went walking with Dublin Kate. The day was brilliant, clear and hot, and as both were putting on weight, they decided to walk to the city and meet their friends down Argent Street.

Patrick O'Hara was tubby, red, volcanic. He knew everyone and was known to all for a downright honest bookmaker, and since it was the day prior to the weekly races, he could not avoid the business thrust upon him. He drank much beer, and although Dublin Kate did not approve of strong drink, she followed O'Hara in and out of pubs and patiently waited for him when he was stopped in the street.

Presently they came to a drinking fountain erected at the kerb-side in memory of a civic father who had owned ten pubs and a distillery. If you must drink water you could press a button and direct your mouth to a spurt of water from the basin, or you could fill a metal cup from a tap. You couldn't take the cup home, pretend it was pewter, and fill it with beer, because it was chained to the fountain.

At the foot of the fountain was a small drinking trough served by a tap below the basin, but long ago a drunk had assaulted the tap, since when it had never functioned.

Patrick O'Hara was about to pass this fountain when Dublin Kate made known her objection to dying of thirst. So he filled the metal cup and emptied it into the trough, and Dublin Kate, knowing nothing of Oliver Twist, asked for more.

Having filled the cup a second time, Patrick O'Hara was about to empty it into the trough when he was accosted by a client, and the bookmaker poised the cup on the edge of the basin. An occasional pedestrian accidentally bumped him and apologised, although O'Hara should have stood on the kerb. These apologies were properly acknowledged, and the bookmaker continued to talk with his client for something like five minutes.

When his client moved on O'Hara emptied the cup of water into the trough and was about to fill it for the third time when again he was saluted by a would-be punter.

"What about Silver Star for the third, Pat?"

"Fives to you," replied O'Hara.

"Suits me for a tenner. Hi! What's the matter with your dog?"

Dublin Kate was slewed sideways as though suffering from a stitch, and abruptly she collapsed into the dry gutter. The astounded O'Hara dropped the cup into the basin, stooped over the body, and swore loudly. A uniformed policeman materialised out of thin air and asked what was going on.

"Can't you ruddy well see?" demanded O'Hara. "Me dog's been poisoned, that's what's going on. I give her a drink of water from the fountain and now look at her."

The policeman happened to be he who had been called by a frantic barman to look at Hans Gromberg, and his actions now obliterated his failure to see the woman who had sat next to Mrs. Wallace. He took position with his back to the fountain, and his feet were angled to guard the moisture in the trough. He ordered the people to move along and then demanded harshly: "What d'you mean, poisoned?"

Two plain-clothes men took charge. The bookmaker related the facts. One detective dissolved into the crowd, and a minute later reappeared from the taxi which drew up beside the fountain. The dead animal was lifted into the taxi and O'Hara told to get in with it. The uniformed policeman went with him to Headquarters.

One of the plain-clothes men guarded the fountain, while the other obtained two files and a wad of blotting paper. The moisture in the trough was mopped up by the blotting paper and the files used to detach the cup from the chain. The foot traffic down Argent Street flowed once again.

Abbot took charge of Patrick O'Hara and the body of Dublin Kate. He listened to the bookmaker's story, his assistant recording it in shorthand. He heard the report of the uniformed man and that of the senior plain-clothes man. It was then four-thirty and Dr. Hoadly's surgery period. A plain-clothes man was sent with the metal cup and the blotting paper, with the request that Dr. Hoadly telephone his opinion even if not substantiated.

Patrick O'Hara was introduced to Bony by Abbot, who placed the statement and the reports on the desk. The bookmaker was told to smoke if he wished, but was so infuriated that he broke four matches in lighting a cigar, and his breathing was a whistling noise in his bulbous nose. He was wearing a single-breasted light grey suit, old but clean. The striped silk shirt was thrust into the background by a brilliant green tie. The shirt was clean, but the tie was stained by what could be tomato soup.

"What age are you, Mr. O'Hara?" Bony asked.

"Age!" gasped the bookmaker. "Why, sixty-four, maybe -five."

"Married?"

"Yes. Twice. Why? What's being married got to do with——"

"Let's take it easy, Mr. O'Hara. Is your second wife alive?"

"No. She died eleven years ago. I'm living with me daughter by me first wife."

"Now I'm going to ask Senior Detective Abbot a routine question which you must not allow to annoy you," Bony went on. "What is Mr. O'Hara's reputation?"

"Good as far as we know, sir," replied Abbot.

"I been in business for twenty-nine years and never at any time——"

"Of course not, Mr. O'Hara. We'll discuss the circumstances concerning the death of your dog. Was it a valuable dog?"

"No value. Too old, but I thought a lot of her. Won a lot of races in her day. Ruddy shame, poisoning her like that. Don't get it."

"We're not certain that she was poisoned," Bony said. "We'll have the report soon, and meanwhile tell me—are you sure that your dog showed no distress after lapping up the first cupful of water?"

"Yes, because it was some time after that I gave her the second cup. A pal of mine bailed me up."

"And you held that second cup of water for some time?"

"Yes, held it on the edge of the basin for two or three minutes. Could have been longer."

"Just show me." Bony moved the inkstand to the edge of the desk. "This is the fountain, and the desk is the roadway. Stand in the position you were when talking to your friend."

The bookmaker complied, and Abbot was placed where the friend stood. The fountain faced to the pavement, and O'Hara's position was partly to one side. He demonstrated how the filled cup had rested on the edge of the basin, and Bony said:

"Naturally, the street being so busy, people bumped you, I suppose?"

"Yes, some of 'em did," agreed O'Hara. "You see, I was caught sort of in a bad position. A bloke bumped me arm and went on, and then another bloke bumped me and gave me a dirty look. After all, it was me own fault. Then a woman sort of knocked me and said she was sorry, and she patted Dublin Kate and said something to her and went on."

"Do you remember that woman?"

The bookmaker scowled, sat down, and glared at the half-consumed cigar.

"Not much. She was getting on. Fiftyish—nearer -one than -nine, I reckon. Had a white hat, I recall that. Dressed——"

A man entered and gave a paper to Abbot, who passed it over the desk to Bony. Bony read: "Doctor telephones is reasonably sure cup has contained cyanide and that blotting paper is saturated with it. Confirmation promised within forty minutes."

"The woman was dressed—Mr. O'Hara?" Bony prompted.

"White hat. I think she was wearing a brown sort of dress."

"What kind of hat—big or ordinary or small—felt or straw?"

"Straw. Bit floppy on one side."

"Spectacles?"

"Don't recollect," replied O'Hara. "You see, I was talking to me friend. Wasn't takin' no notice of anyone else."

"And she stopped to pat the dog, you say?"

"Yes. She went round my friend to do that, as Dublin Kate was standing in the gutter to keep out of the way."

"Did she have a handbag?"

"Yes, she had a handbag. I remember seeing that. Tucked under her arm when she patted Kate. Blue handbag with red handles."

"What kind of handles?"

Mr. O'Hara was hurt. This questioning seemed so futile.

"Kind of handles?" he returned. "Why, ordinary floppy sort of handles, of course. Looked like leather or something."

"Abbot! Middle-aged woman. White straw hat, brown dress, blue handbag with red handles or drawstrings. Probably still in Argent Street."

Abbot sped down the corridor. The bookmaker was decidedly pale. Bony was as smooth as ever when he said:

"Mr. O'Hara, I want you to go home and stay there until I call for you. Name of the man you were talking to?"

"Ted Rowe. Licensee of Camel Camp Hotel, North B.H. Why do I have to stay at home? Races to-morrow. Must be there——"

"Then drink nothing unless out of a bottle." Bony made for the door. "Come on! Off you go!"

"But what's it mean? What's the idea?"

Bony took the man by the arm and urged him out to the corridor.

"You heard about Sam Goldspink? Go home and stay there."

There were men in the public office. Pavier was with them. Bony edged Patrick O'Hara past them. He had to open the door for the bookmaker. Having closed the door, he turned about to hear the Superintendent giving orders. Two men to examine every tram leaving Argent Street at the south end and two to examine trams leaving by the other. Men to visit every shop on both sides of the street, and others to 'go through' every hotel.

All left together, Pavier and Bony with them. It was a full hour since Dublin Kate had died.

There would be other police in the street to be alerted. A blue handbag with red drawstrings in possession of a woman in a white 'floppy' straw hat. White hats are noticeable, and so are handbags having red handles—drawstrings. But Bony was not hopeful. After attempting that murder the woman would be unlikely to linger in the city.

Bony walked smartly down Argent Street. The number of women wearing white hats—felt, straw, small, large, stiff, floppy—was remarkable. Blue, red, white, green, grey handbags, but not the blue bag with the red drawstrings. Halfway down Argent Street he saw Mary Isaacs outside a hotel. She was obviously excited, almost 'dancing with excitement'. Seeing him, she ran to meet him.

"She's in there. I saw her go in," she cried, and clung with both hands to Bony's arm. "A customer wanted an article in the window, and I went outside with her to see what it was. Then I saw the woman with the blue bag with red strings. She was coming this way and I hurried after her. I left the customer and followed her. I don't know what Mrs. Robinov will say. She went in there—that woman."

"See her face?"

"No. All I saw was her back. Brown frock. White hat. Seemed taller than I remembered. It was the bag, Inspector. I'm sure it was the bag."

"You return to the shop," Bony said, and had to remove her hands from his arm. "Leave it to us. Mrs. Robinov will understand."

Beside the main entrance there were four bar and lounge doors, and Bony remained with his back to the traffic to watch all of them. Minutes passed before two plain-clothes men approached, and Bony stopped them and related what he had been told.

"The Super and the senior's on the other side of the street, sir," one said.

"Bring them over."

The man hurried across the street, and to the other Bony said:

"A back entrance, I suppose?"

"Yes, sir. Into a lane running parallel. Shall I block it?"

Bony nodded, and the man vanished into a doorway. Pavier and Abbot arrived, and to them Bony repeated Mary's story.

Leaving the plain-clothes man outside, they went through the lounges systematically, and even the bars. Accompanied by the manager, they searched the upper rooms. The manager's wife and two maids searched the retiring rooms. Even the domestic quarters and rear yard buildings were searched. No woman as described by Patrick O'Hara.

From the hotel to Goldspink's shop was about a hundred yards, and when the shops either side the hotel had been investigated, Bony proceeded to interview Mary Isaacs. The shop was full of customers, and he was discreetly conducted to the fitting-room and Mary brought to him.

"You didn't see her face, you said, Mary?" Bony asked.

"No, sir. Did you find her?"

"Not a sign of her. How far behind the woman were you when you followed her?"

"Only two or three yards."

"She didn't turn to see if she were being followed?"

"No. But she might have seen me following her by looking in the shop windows. I was frantic. I couldn't see a policeman to tell."

Bony patted her shoulder and managed to chuckle.

"They say you never can find a policeman when you want one. Well, it was a good try. You did fine, and the police will catch her before she leaves Argent Street. I won't keep you. Mrs. Robinov will need you in the shop —they're so busy."

It was nearing six o'clock—O Dreaded Hour! The pavement was packed, the street traffic heavy. A trifle despondent, Bony sauntered back towards Headquarters.

It would be stupid to doubt that a lunatic walked Argent Street: and all things were possible to lunatic Tuttaway—the famed magician, the quick-change artist, the master of female impersonation. Dressed as that woman, had he seen reflected by the shop windows the girl from Goldspink's shop, recognised her, noted her agitation? Had he walked into the hotel, gone directly to a retiring-room, and emerged with his clothes reversed, the trick handbag reversed and the straw hat crushed within it? The evidence was against this, but . . .

A man fell into step with him.

"Just got word, sir, that the wanted woman has been picked up and taken to Headquarters."

CHAPTER SEVENTEEN

A Stage with Coffee

"This is the life! Be ready in two ticks."

Mrs. Wallace did remarkably well, just under ten minutes, and she settled herself in the back seat of the police car as though off to a civic reception. Seated with her, Abbot talked of the weather.

Meanwhile Bony faced a difficulty with Superintendent Pavier, in whose office sat the woman brought in by two detectives who had worked the trams. The woman was dressed as described by Patrick O'Hara, and her handbag was blue. But the red handles were of thick cord, and the bag was not the drawstring type.

Moreover the woman readily admitted stopping at the street fountain and patting the unfortunate dog. She gave her name as Sandra Goddard, living with her husband in South Broken Hill, where they conducted a grocery and wood-and-oil store.

"We've made a bloomer," Pavier stonily admitted.

"How old do you think she is?" asked Bony.

"Under forty, I'd say."

"Any children?"

"Didn't ask her. Important?"

"Could be. I'd like to see the contents of her handbag. You come along and leave the questions to me."

On their way, Bony learned from Pavier what information had already been gleaned, and when they entered the Superintendent's office the new secretary rose from her chair to leave at a nod from her Chief.

Only in figure was Mrs. Goddard similar to the woman described by Mrs. Wallace, supported by Mrs. Lucas. She was certainly not more than forty. Bony was presented as Inspector Knapp, and, having become seated, he proceeded to soothe.

"We are really regretful, Mrs. Goddard, at having inconvenienced you," he said, presenting a box of Bond Street cigarettes.

"Well, it's a beastly nuisance," the woman fumed. "Besides being dragged here like a criminal. I don't know what my husband will have to say about it. Thank you."

"I do think, Mrs. Goddard, that when I've explained the circumstances you will forgive us. Could I ask you to treat in strict confidence what I would like to tell you?"

A secret! A secret to a woman is like fish to a starved cat. A favour sought by a debonair, good-looking man with wonderful blue eyes and such a voice! Then Bony smiled, and annoyance vanished.

"Of course, Inspector. I promise."

"Well, it is this. The dog you petted at the fountain died a few minutes after you left. She drank water from the trough at the foot of the fountain, and the water was poisoned. The owner of the dog is a Mr. Patrick O'Hara, who, being fond of the animal, was very aggrieved. He remembered you patting the dog, and we thought you had something to do with its sudden death.

An unfortunate mistake, but one brought about by over-zeal. By the way, you live at Number 1 Willow Street, South Broken Hill. In business there, I understand?"

"We are. I manage the grocery store and my husband runs the wood-and-oil business. We've been there for eight years now."

"Family, I suppose?"

"No, we haven't any children—not living. I had a little boy, but he died when he was two."

"A sad blow, Mrs. Goddard. Being the father of three boys, I can offer sympathy with sincerity. I won't keep you more than another minute. Would you like to be taken home in one of our cars?"

"It would save time, and my husband will be wanting his dinner."

"Being a mere policeman," Bony went on, "there are occasions on which I cannot be a gentleman. Suspicious to the very end, and all that kind of thing. No doubt you have already allied the death of the dog this afternoon with the death of several men."

"I couldn't help but do that," Mrs. Goddard admitted, a frown deepening the lines between her eyes.

"I do dislike having to ask you," lied Bony. "Would you let me look into your handbag?"

Mrs. Goddard offered no objection—and the handbag. It was, of course, navy blue. The handles were of red cord, and the bag was fastened by clips. The contents were normal and limited. There was certainly no cyanide—and no baby's dummy. Bony carefully restored the articles, closed the bag, and proffered it to its owner.

"I am thankful that nasty little suspicion of mine is smashed," he said smilingly. "And very grateful indeed for your generosity in return for our silly mistake. Permit me to conduct you to the car."

Superintendent Pavier came round his desk to offer his hand and also expressed his regrets, and Mrs. Goddard, obviously mollified, left the office with Bony. In the Public Office they had to pass Mrs. Wallace, who, after one swift glance at the navy-blue handbag, said:

"Why, Mrs. Goddard! How's things? Haven't seen you for ages."

"How are you, Mrs. Wallace? No, I don't get out much during the day. The shop keeps me tied."

Bony paused while the women chatted for a few moments and then led Mrs. Goddard to the waiting police car drawn up behind that which had brought Mrs. Wallace. The driver opened the door. Mrs. Goddard smiled, and Bony bowed.

"*Au revoir*," he murmured. "Should I think of any way in which you could assist me, you would call again?"

"Certainly. We are law-abiding citizens, you know," replied Mrs. Goddard. "You'll find our number in the telephone book."

Bony stepped back and the car moved off.

When he returned to Mrs. Wallace she said conspiratorially:

"That can't be her, Inspector. I'd have spotted Mrs. Goddard in that lounge. She and that woman are the same height, same build, and she's got the same hennaed hair like that woman. But . . . But it couldn't have been Mrs. Goddard."

"You have known Mrs. Goddard long?"

"Couple of years, I suppose. Haven't seen her for six

months before to-day, though. But it couldn't have been her, Inspector."

When she had gone, Pavier appeared.

"Hoadly's analysis proves it was cyanide in that metal cup and on the blotting paper," he said. "Come home to dinner and talk."

"Thanks, Super. I'd like to."

"All right. Car's at the back."

"Just how far have you progressed?" Pavier asked when they were on the road. Bony hesitated, and the Superintendent said with strange inelegance: "I won't cook your pork and beans."

Bony gave in.

"The oddities are so many that the pattern will not emerge clearly, Super. And with all the forces you have placed at my service I am unable to make it emerge. Two men have been poisoned in the same way. They were both elderly and both unmarried. There is a third similarity, which is that both men were murdered on a Friday afternoon.

"The poisoning of the third man gave much and strengthened confirmation of theories. It gave us a description of a woman who could have dropped cyanide into the man's beer. Like the first two, the third victim was also unmarried and elderly, but the third man wasn't poisoned on a Friday afternoon. Finally we have the attempt to poison O'Hara on a Friday afternoon. But O'Hara was twice married. The two common denominators are that those four men are elderly and they are not careful of their clothes when at table.

"Leaving out the O'Hara case, a woman seems to be associated with the three poisonings. In two of those cases we have a particular type of handbag to support the belief. Through a glass darkly, therefore, we see the dim shape of a woman.

"Motive? Apparently there isn't one. But of course there is a motive. There must be. As I pointed out to Crome or Abbot, it could be that the series of murders is meant to hide the motive for the murder of but one man. So far we have nothing to prove or disprove that idea."

"You aren't sure that the poisoner is a woman?" interposed Pavier.

"I can be sure of nothing," admitted Bony. "I am inclined to the belief that it's a woman."

Pavier purposely drove slowly, and presently Bony said:

"After Goldspink was poisoned, Crome and his men tapped all the sources of supply of cyanide in Broken Hill. After Parsons died, Crome and his men doubled their efforts and were spurred on by Stillman. Since Gromberg was poisoned, all that work was done over again. Results nil. As you know, commercial cyanide is sold to stations and country stores in two-, three-, and seven-pound tins, and our poisoner would require much less than a two-pound tin to start operations.

"We think a woman is the poisoner, but after to-day I am inclined to consider that it might be a man. Tuttaway escaped on September twenty-seventh, and Goldspink was murdered a month later, that murder being the first of the series.

"The woman followed by Mary Isaacs entered a hotel which we searched five minutes after she went in, and she had vanished. The Great Scarsby could have rung the changes with clothes and handbag, having seen his follower reflected by shop windows. And yet, artist though he was, I doubt if he would have deceived a woman like Mrs. Wallace, an ex-barmaid who knows all the answers, as the saying goes. Simple isn't it?"

"Still, you have made decided headway," Pavier said approvingly. "You've got far beyond where Stillman left off."

"That is to be expected," blandly agreed Bony. "The final touch of confusion is that Tuttaway is also careless at table."

"What!"

Bony avoided explanation on this point, saying:

"I hope you will continue to approve of the road blocks?"

"I'll keep them there until you ask for their removal."

"Thanks."

A few minutes later Bony was being presented to Pavier's sister, who managed his house, and then Luke appeared, to suggest a 'snort' before dinner.

That dinner was to linger in Bony's memory. The red glow of the sunset seeped through the open windows to gleam on the cutlery and crystal and tint faintly red the solitary diamond on his hostess's finger. Birds chirped in the pepper tree beyond, their voices triumphant over the rumble of the distant mines.

There was no 'shop'. The elder Pavier talked books, and the son almost shyly admitted to writing plays.

"Haven't been successful so far," he said candidly. "But I'm hoping."

"But you have," argued his aunt. "You had a play staged last August."

"That's not success," Luke argued, and explained to the guest that one of his plays had been twice performed in aid of charity.

"It was so well done, Mr. Bonaparte, that several hundred pounds were raised," the aunt declared. "The local talent is very good. Everyone thoroughly enjoyed it. I'm sure Luke will show you his miniature stage after dinner. It's fun. I help him move the various characters about."

The stage was brought in with the coffee and set up on the table. The technique was explained to Bony, who was interested in any subject presented by people knowing something of it. It was evident that Luke's knowledge of plays and players was extensive, and that his enthusiasm was hot, but after half an hour Bony was dismayed by his own ignorance.

"What kind of shows were staged by the Great Scarsby?" he asked.

"Scarsby!" Luke shot a swift glance at his father, as though for permission to discuss 'shop'. "The Great Scarsby, and the Great Martini, and the Great Lafayette depended largely on spectacle to achieve effects. For instance, the Great Lafayette had an easel put up and a canvas placed on it. He smashed a hole in the canvas, and from behind the easel a Nubian thrust his face into the hole. Lafayette slapped whiskers on the black man's face, painted him with white and pink wash, and stood back to reveal a portrait of Edward VII. Then he went behind the easel—and the Nubian stepped away and came round to the front, tore off the whiskers and wiped his face, and there stood Lafayette himself."

"Clever," agreed Bony. "He could, I suppose, change

his clothes quickly—and that kind of thing?"

"Walk behind a mirror and emerge as a woman wearing an evening frock, disappear and come again as Queen Victoria, go round once again behind the mirror and reappear as a well-known statesman. And he wouldn't be behind the mirror longer than it would take him to walk from one side to the other."

"You saw this act?"

"Oh no. I was only a kid when Lafayette died in a theatre fire in Edinburgh—trying to save a wonderful white horse. Some say that Scarsby was his equal, none that he was superior to Lafayette in the show business."

Following dinner Bony left with Pavier, who wanted to return to his office. Luke accompanied them to the car, and it seemed that he felt he could talk shop outside the house.

"That picture you have," he said to Bony, "it recalled to mind someone I knew, and I couldn't place her. Remember?"

"Of course."

"There's something about that woman strongly resembling a woman who acted in my play and who I thought was the best of the lot of us. The name's Goddard, and she lives at Number 1 Willow Street."

"In what particular does she resemble the picture?" asked Bony, and Pavier stood motionless.

"Mouth and chin. Mean anything?"

"What were you doing late this afternoon?"

"Been home since four. Why—Mr. Friend?"

Bony laughed, and the Superintendent said:

"Thank heaven for that."

CHAPTER EIGHTEEN

Inspector Bonaparte to Jimmy Nimmo

At the time Mrs. Goddard boarded a tram in Argent Street, Mary Isaacs was following a woman carrying a well-remembered handbag. Superficially that proved that Mrs. Goddard was not the woman seen and followed to the hotel by Mary Isaacs, and had it not been for the doubt in the mind of Mrs. Wallace after meeting Mrs. Goddard, and for the resemblance to Mrs. Goddard Luke Pavier saw in Mills's picture done under the supervision of both Mrs. Wallace and Mrs. Lucas, Bony might have been satisfied.

He telephoned for Jimmy Nimmo, and within half an hour Jimmy was seated before his desk.

"There are people named Goddard, man and wife, no family, in business at Number 1 Willow Street, South Broken Hill. You don't happen to know them or of them?"

"Of them, yes," replied Jimmy. "They run a grocery store and fuel yard. House behind the store. Big woodyard. Every Saturday night they come to town to go to the pictures, leaving two lights on in the house to bluff poor innocent burglars."

"Ah! You have surveyed the scene, it would appear."

"Had it mapped out before luck wiped me."

"When was that, Jimmy?"

"When we met down Argent Street."

"Come now, don't be so unkind," Bony objected. "You have on several occasions referred to the 'attraction'. Surely that was not brought about by lack of luck."

"It comes into it," protested Jimmy. "I'm getting married some time soon, and I'll have to retire to keep the peace. Couldn't bear to be in the jug and another fella taking my missus around. Women oughta have a man handy to keep them straight."

"Too bad, Jimmy. Because I want you to undertake a little burglary for me. Being Saturday, I want you to enter Number 1 Willow Street and search for a navy-blue handbag with red drawstrings, a baby's dummy, and a quantity of cyanide. I shall be working here late to-night to receive your report before going off to bed."

"Supposin' I get pinched? All me good intentions gone west, and married love done in the eye."

"You won't be pinched—unless you should disobey my orders by lifting money or some article of negotiable value. You will be working for me, Jimmy, and I am the police."

"Well, can I tell me wench I'm workin' for the police —meaning you? I got to square off for not taking her to the pictures."

"Can she keep a secret?"

"Good as I can. Not the sort to let her right know what her left's doing—like me."

"Very well. That's agreed. I'll see that you are not apprehended, but you will take as much care in entering and leaving as though ten policemen were on the look-out for you."

"Righto! I'll be seein' you."

Bony went along to Crome's room, where he asked for the file on Tuttaway, and mentioned that it would be helpful of Inspector Hobson if between 8 and 11 P.M. his man on patrol in the vicinity of Willow Street would not approach Number 1. Crome said he would fix it.

"Any line on Tuttaway, sir?" he asked, presenting the required file.

"Afraid not," replied Bony. "I think he may be walking about Broken Hill in the complete freedom of a perfect disguise. What are you doing this morning?"

"I'm taking out those three trackers to have another look around for the haft of that glass knife."

"Good! I won't detain you."

Bony took the file back to his room. It was fairly sketchy before the crime for which Tuttaway had been imprisoned, giving date of birth and biographical details of his career. The medical history was equally vague prior to the conviction, and this pre-trial information had been supplied by London.

Tuttaway was the second of a family of four sons and four daughters. Two sons had taken over their father's business, and one had subsequently suicided. Of the four daughters, one had married a minister, another an artist, yet another had married an architect and within a year had to be certified. The remaining daughter had been associated with the magician brother. All the Tuttaways had inherited much money.

Bony regarded the picture taken by the prison authorities. It was a strange face, the tottering mind emphasising and revealing. Nobility and evil, ruthlessness and generosity, humour and arrogance. Being an actor, a showman, a man controlled utterly by his own egotism, Tuttaway's greatest enemy was Tuttaway. He must have occupied a place, great or small, in the life of the woman he murdered. She must have known him at some period of her life prior to coming to Broken Hill or leaving England. That must be it: prior to leaving England in June 1936.

Yet her sister had repeatedly affirmed that Muriel Lodding had not been interested in men. Mrs. Dalton had . . .

"Mrs. Dalton is here, sir," said Senior Detective Abbot. "She wanted to see the Super, but he's out, and so's Sergeant Crome."

"Tell her that I will be pleased to do what I can for her," purred Bony.

Bony blew cigarette ash off the desk top, slid the Tuttaway file into a drawer, and swiftly rearranged papers. He was standing when Mrs. Dalton was shown in, and he was presented to a woman instantly pleasing. Brown hair softly rolled at the nape of her neck, and the narrow upturned brim of the small hat added even more expression to the expressive grey eyes. Her nose was Grecian, and the make-up not obvious, save the lipstick, which reflected the cyclamen shade of the printed frock beneath the flowing black coat. Her accessories were all black.

"Mrs. Dalton! Do sit down. I am Inspector Knapp. Perhaps I can be of service?"

Her eyes registered momentary surprise and then approval.

"I called to see Superintendent Pavier about my sister," she said. "Muriel left all her small estate to me and also appointed me her executrix. I received a letter from Superintendent Pavier concerning salary and accrued leave pay owing to her. I've brought the will. Her solicitor's name and address are shown on it."

Bony accepted the proffered document.

"I'm sorry the Superintendent isn't in," he said, noting the name and address of the solicitor and returning the will. "The department will communicate with your sister's solicitor. Opinion here of Miss Lodding was very high, Mrs. Dalton. I didn't have the opportunity to know her very well, but Superintendent Pavier feels he has suffered a personal loss."

"She loved working here: said the work was much more exciting than in a broker's office."

"She—you have no relatives—in Australia?"

"In Australia, no. In England there are several cousins, but neither of us corresponded with them. My husband died years ago, and we have no children."

"You have, I understand, lived in Broken Hill for several years?"

"Yes, since 1938. I never liked Sydney, too frightfully humid, and when my sister was asked to transfer to the Broken Hill office of her firm, I came with her. We both like living here, although cultural interests are few. Do you happen to be investigating my sister's death?"

"Well, yes, I am working with Detective Sergeant Crome," Bony answered. "We shall, of course, find Tuttaway."

"You are certain it was he who killed her?"

"Quite. Your sister must have known him, surely. Probably when you were living in England."

"Yes. That's my second reason for coming to Superintendent Pavier. Although the man's name was familiar —for who hasn't heard of the Great Scarsby?—I didn't recall that my sister had had any contact with him.

"You see, Inspector, it's all of fourteen years since we left England, and I'm not sure but I think Tuttaway was then in America. And then when he was imprisoned for abducting that girl, we were living here, and my sister evinced no great interest in the case, excepting to recall that at one time or another she had done some work for him. But I suppose that won't be of much help."

"On the contrary, Mrs. Dalton, it may be of extreme importance. Do go on."

"Well, then, I must tell you something of our life before we left London. Do you mind?"

Mrs. Dalton produced a cigarette-case from her hand-bag, and, when holding a match in service, Bony murmured:

"London! I've always wanted to see London. Once I had the opportunity of exchange duty, but it didn't come off. What part of London did you live in?"

"Ealing. Quite close to the Underground—Gosport Grove. Far enough from the city to be out of the traffic noises and yet within easy reach. My husband left me comfortably well off, and Muriel had no need to work, but she insisted on doing something. She then worked for several authors, typing their manuscripts and assisting them generally, and she would never discuss her work or her clients other than to mention their names.

"It wasn't as though they came to my house. Muriel either went to their houses or brought their work home, and I never sought to know more of them than she cared to tell me. I was thinking about this last night when I remembered that my sister once did work for the Great Scarsby, and the name came to my mind only because Muriel mentioned that his work was more difficult than the other. And now——"

"We are convinced that it was Tuttaway who was seen with your sister that last evening of her life. We know for certain that Tuttaway was in Broken Hill that night and think he is still in Broken Hill. Can you recall anything more of that association of your sister with the Great Scarsby?"

"No, I'm afraid not, Inspector. You see, it's all so very vague, and at the time so unimportant. What I am sure about is that there was no love affair between them. Why, she must have been twenty or twenty-five years his junior."

"Can you recall when, what year, your sister did work for George Henry Tuttaway?"

"Well, it must have been before he went to America in 1934. I don't know—it could be—no, Inspector, I'm afraid I cannot answer your question."

"You have no reason to fear he might be, shall we say, interested in you?"

"In me! Why should he be? I am a little afraid, however, that when caught he may tell hi___ stories about Muriel. Why he ___ I'm sure the police woul___ ravings, but the newspa___ publicity. Muriel was so___ She used to tell me sh___

Bony stopped doodli___ couragingly at Mrs. D___

"You need have no cause for concern," he told her. "Tuttaway, having been certified and having escaped from custody, will not be charged with murdering your sister, because he is unfit to stand trial."

"He will merely be returned to the prison?" Mrs. Dalton asked bitterly, and rose to leave.

"That will be the result of his apprehension."

"I hope you will prove him guilty. It won't lessen my loneliness, but I want to know the truth." Her lips trembled and her eyes filled with tears. "I miss my sister very much and think I won't be able to stay in Broken Hill. We understood each other so completely, and all our interests were the same. Do you think that Scarsby is also responsible for those other murders?"

"It's possible, Mrs. Dalton, but we have as yet no proof. Just leave the worrying to me. We'll find him. We always get our man, you know."

"I hope so. But the police didn't catch Jack the Ripper, did they?"

"Ah! But I wasn't in London."

"Of course not." Mrs. Dalton tried to smile. "I forgot you were never in London. Well, good-bye. You'll tell Superintendent Pavier I called?"

"Oh yes. And about the money owing your sister's estate. Good-bye, Mrs. Dalton. I am so glad the Superintendent was out."

CHAPTER NINETEEN

Unprofessional Conduct

The Lodding case now gave promise of breaking, but the poisoning cases refused to give.

The connection between Muriel Lodding and George Henry Tuttaway, established by Mrs. Dalton, was a distinct advance. The murder had been prompted by a reason born in the past and was not the result of swift passion or blood lust. Therefore the odds were against another murder by the Great Scarsby.

Bony discussed Tuttaway with Crome late that afternoon.

"Had a visit from Mrs. Dalton this morning," he said, offering a slip of paper. "That's the name and address of Muriel Lodding's solicitors. You might pass it on to Finance Section."

"What do you think of her?"

"Mrs. Dalton? Cultured. Very much alive. The sister knew Tuttaway in England."

"Is that so?" exclaimed Crome with great satisfaction.

Bony related what Mrs. Dalton had told him, and Crome pounced on the fact that, Tuttaway's motive having been born in the past, it was unlikely that he had stayed one unnecessary moment in Broken Hill.

"Think we could lift those road blocks now?" he suggested. "Bit of a strain on the department."

"Wait, Crome. For the time being we'll act on the Emperor's advice : 'When in doubt do nothing.' Meanwhile, make a few notes.

"In 1934 Tuttaway took a company on tour through the United States. At that time Muriel Lodding was living with her sister at Gosport Grove, Ealing, London, and was engaged by several authors in preparing their manuscripts. Note that Lodding did this work at Mrs. Dalton's house and that she visited her clients and not they her. An additional client was Tuttaway, and, like the writers, he did not appear at the house.

"Two years after Tuttaway went off to America the sisters came to Australia, and in the following year Tuttaway also came to Australia, having disbanded his company. That was in '37. The next year, in November, the sisters left Sydney and came to Broken Hill—we understand because a better position became available here in Lodding's firm.

"That may be the reason behind the move to Broken Hill, or it may have been dictated by the appearance of Tuttaway on the Lodding Sydney scene. The point will have to be checked. Did Lodding ask for that transfer to Broken Hill, or was it offered her? Ask Sydney to check up with the wool firm and dig out all that can be obtained concerning the two women. Records have the addresses."

Crome was faintly perplexed.

"Suppose it's necessary, sir?" he asked. "Considering that it was Tuttaway who killed Lodding?"

"I think so," Bony replied coldly. "Further, have Sydney ask London for the number of the house in Gosport Grove, Ealing, occupied by Mrs. Dalton prior to 1936, and for any information re the lives and associations of the two sisters."

"Very well, sir," Crome said stoically.

"We could obtain most of this from Mrs. Dalton, but we won't bother her too much just now. The life of Muriel Lodding before coming to Broken Hill is most important, and it will give Sydney something to think about and remove the idea from their minds that Broken Hill is doing nothing.

"You still hold the ball," Bony went on. "Until we know to the contrary we must think Tuttaway is in Broken Hill. By the way, when making your report to the Super, keep in mind that you are acting on your own initiative and that I am fully occupied by the cyanide murders."

Crome flushed, nodded grateful understanding, and left. Like many another man, Bill Crome had emerged from rigorous training as an efficient member of a machine oiled by regulations and fuelled by directives. He dared never thumb his nose at those higher up, for he lacked independence and the instinct of knowing the right moment. As a member of a team, he pulled his weight, which is why teamwork is of such value in modern crime investigation.

Bony slipped the top sheet from the blotter, regarded the doodling he had done when listening to Mrs. Dalton, and tossed the sheet into the w.p.b. He collected his hat and sauntered along the corridor to the general office of the Detective Branch, spoke to Abbot, and stood before the black-and-white drawings of the woman described by Mrs. Wallace and Mrs. Lucas. A trifle despondent, he walked to his hotel for dinner.

Jimmy Nimmo reported at eleven. He was wearing a loose-fitting dark brown suit and crêpe-soled shoes, and, having made himself at ease and lit a cigarette, he began without preamble.

"I went at eight and stayed till half-past ten. No hand-bag and no baby's dummy, either." Professional pride carried him onward, as though the absence of results was an admission of failure. "I went through that joint from shop to yard office. I looked under counters and in drawers. The till was empty and the bacon cutter wants cleaning. Behind the shop are two bedrooms, a living-room, a lounge, and a kitchen with a small wash-house behind it. One of the bedrooms is occupied by the parties, the other's a spare.

"Under the bed is a large tin box you can buy from Disposals. It was locked, but the lock's the kind the old man gave me to play with when I was five. In the box are two .38 automatics and two hundred-odd rounds of ammunition. Also about four thousand useless petrol tickets.

"Nothing much in the lounge exceptin' a hole in the wall behind a glass-front bookcase, and in the hole there just had to be a safe. I decided to risk ten minutes, and fluked it. In the safe is plenty—cash, bank passbooks, and forty-eight gold wrist watches.

"The kitchen had something too. Under a loose floor-board there's another tin box a bit smaller than the one in the bedroom, and in it a cashbox holding between seven hundred and a thousand quid. In spite of what you're thinking, I couldn't have cared less. Besides the cashbox is a bundle of letters and, remembering that you used to nose into other people's letters, I read a couple. Addressed to Mrs. Madge Goddard, aimed at 'Darling Madge by Your Everlasting Arty'. What's the husband's name?"

"Frederick Albert."

Jimmy grinned widely. "Extra to the letters is a black golliwog and nine photographs of a small kid. The love letters being in that box with all the money indicates that the husband don't know about it. The cash musta been milked from the shop takings to beat the husband or the income tax—the husband, I'll bet."

"You looked under the wardrobe and on top of it?"

"Be easy, Inspector. The bag isn't in that house, and there's no baby. There's two handbags, a snakeskin bag and a black silk affair. Both empty. I poked into everything. Nothing like poison anywhere in the house.

"There's a manhole in the kitchen, and I took a bird's-eye under the roof. Nothing but dust and spiders. So I went out back to take a decko inside the woodyard office. The office is built into one end of the back veranda of the house, and the door has a Yale-type lock I don't bother with. I found a loose sheet of iron in the roof and went in that way.

"The office isn't so big but pretty crowded. Usual things, ledgers, files, and docket books. On the wall is two Winchester rifles, a Savage high-powered weapon, and a shotgun. All well kept. Boxes of ammunition on a shelf. In a corner is a stack of kangaroo skins. On another shelf there's five seven-pound tins of cyanide and a cardboard box containing at some time a round dozen bottles of white strychnine crystals. In the box now are four untapped bottles and one partly used.

There's a stack of docket books going back for two years, and that's the lot."

"Quite a catalogue," Bony said approvingly. "D'you know anything of kangaroo hunting?"

"Not a thing, but I've never heard of feedin' them with cyanide and hitting 'em in the eye with a bottle of strychnine. Have you?"

"Cyanide is used extensively, however, in keeping down rabbits and other vermin."

Jimmy lit another cigarette.

"You know, Inspector, I think the state ought to hire me at two thousand quid a year just to amble around people's houses. No need to pinch anything, and I could live me natural life. Think of the interestin' things I'd find for government departments—Taxation, Customs, Health. And the police. Read the other day that writers in Russia are best paid in the world. Why don't Australia use up burglars like Russia uses up their writers? A good dozen burglars would wipe out all the rackets."

"I have had the idea, Jimmy, for a considerable time," Bony said, his eyes twinkling. "But Australia being a nation of knockers, I would certainly be knocked down did I suggest it in official quarters. There are decided weaknesses too. I also read the article you refer to, and you will remember that the Russian writer who doesn't keep strictly to the Party line is very soon retired. How many burglars could keep the lawful line, even at two thousand a year? Know where I can buy a glass dagger?"

"Can't say I do. Never seen one. Feller told me he saw one in the fist of a Negro soldier. Got anything on the old-fashioned bright steel kind?"

"It seems that the blade of a glass dagger can be filed near the haft and broken off when in the wound, to stop bleeding."

"Neat, Inspector." Jimmy stared pensively at Bony. "The papers didn't say it was a glass dagger."

"That is so. Other than tampering with the blade for the purpose I mentioned, I cannot see any advantages."

"Coloured?"

"Blue."

"Ask the Great Scarsby. I've seen fellas like him throw coloured daggers at dames on the stage."

"That, I think, was the original use for the knife which killed the Lodding woman. We haven't found the haft yet. When taking your day-time constitutional, keep on the look-out for it. You don't know of any likely hide-outs Tuttaway could tenant, I suppose?"

"Fair go, Inspector. Those I did know have been pretty thoroughly probed by Crome and his boys. Must be slick as hell rigging himself up. Wish I had his know-how. When are you letting me out?"

"Still pining?"

"There's that sick aunt, you know."

"And the attraction?"

"And the attraction. Wants to see my police badge. You got one to spare?"

"Never possessed one, Jimmy. Fixed a date for the wedding?"

"No, she keeps backing and filling."

"Strange. You should make a very successful shop-walker."

Jimmy was plainly startled.

"She told you?" he asked.

"No. It's my own opinion. I hope your intentions are strictly honourable?"

"They're damned unprofessional," snorted Jimmy the Screwsman. "I get an eyeful of the pearls and diamonds, and then you butt in and say: 'Oh no, you must not. You don't disconnect them burglar alarms, and you don't withdraw those trinkets from their velvet beds.' Then, when I make up me mind that I'm keener on the dame than the jewels, and she falls for me, you say that I aim to marry her for 'em. Why must you demons always be so damned suspicious?"

"I am wondering, Jimmy."

"What in hell about?"

"Whether you are being driven by love or avarice." Jimmy heaved up to his feet.

"What d'you think?" he almost shouted, and indignation told its tale. "Good night!"

"I'll see you out," Bony said, and accompanied the burglar along the corridor. His shoes resounded on the bare floor; Jimmy's feet made no more noise than a cat's paw. At the door Bony paused.

"The best of luck, Jimmy. I mean that."

CHAPTER TWENTY

To Court a Maid

Ted Pluto was a Darling River aborigine and quite a smart fellow. He could read comic strips and the sporting papers, and he could write and even work out the simpler crossword puzzles. Naturally, he was a fine horseman and a fairly reliable stockman.

Ted liked Broken Hill. He liked working for the police as black tracker, horse breaker, car-washer, and handy man at the lock-up. Since he was only twenty, it could be expected that he would soon tire of the city and its white people and suffer unbearable nostalgia for the bush and the maidens of his own race, but then Chic Chic was the city magnet for Ted Pluto.

Chic Chic was eighteen and beautiful, and the Reverend Playfair quite a good sort, provided a fellow did his courting openly and in daylight. Thus it was that every Sunday afternoon Ted Pluto walked to the Manse, escorted Chic Chic to Sunday school and back to the Manse to eat quantities of sweet cakes in the kitchen with Chic Chic after she had taken afternoon tea to the Reverend and Mrs. Playfair.

These visits demanded much attention to dress, and this Sunday, as usual, Ted Pluto asked Sergeant Crome for leave of absence and left the Headquarters with his mind cleaned like a slate of everything connected with it. Even the glass dagger.

The haft of the glass dagger had become an object of great importance to Ted Pluto, as to the other trackers. He had contributed to the story of the man who had carried a dead woman across sandy ground to the foot of a mullock dump, and he had been shown the blade of the dagger, cleaned of blood, and translucent blue when held before the sun.

With the other trackers and Sergeant Crome, Ted Pluto had hunted for the missing dagger haft, and he had quickly made up his mind that it wasn't to be found in that section of waste ground. Nevertheless, Sergeant Crome had ordered him to continue the search, and to please the boss he and the other trackers had done so. Finally the sergeant had promised a pound of tobacco to the tracker who found the haft which fitted the glass blade.

Dressed in gabardine trousers and white silk shirt, and with gleaming brown shoes on his slightly pigeon-toed feet, and with a pretty face in the offing, who the heck wanted to remember glass daggers with or without hafts?

He was some distance from the Manse when he saw a group of white children playing, and the game they played so captivated him that he actually forgot that Chic Chic would be waiting.

A small boy and a smaller girl were sauntering along the pavement. The boy carried a stick as, doubtless, he had seen a Regency Buck so doing on the screen. The little girl trod daintily at his side, over her arm a narrow sheepskin hanging to represent a fur. She had brilliant red hair and wore a clean print frock, and from about her neck was suspended a shining 'gem'.

Out of their sight, round the corner of a low iron fence, lurked three desperadoes, one armed with a pistol, and, on the lady and her escort arriving at the corner, they jumped out, shouting:

"Stick 'em up!"

The gentleman employed his stick as a sword, whereupon the gunman shouted "Bang!" and the gentleman realistically sagged at the knees and collapsed in the best cinema style. The desperadoes proceeded to surround the lady, and the gunman shouted:

"Come on, now, hand over that jool or you'll get it too. This is a stick-up, lady, an' we're desperate men."

As the gunman's accomplices were holding tightly to the lady's arms, it was not possible for her to obey, and the gunman clenched his teeth about the pistol and jerked the 'jool' upward to free the neck string from the lady's head. The three then decamped, and the dead gentleman raised himself to one knee, groaned with agony, lifted his stick like a rifle, and yelled thrice "Bang!" He proved to be an excellent shot, for one after another the robbers fell down lifeless.

That concluded the game. The children gathered into a bunch, and the boys proceeded to argue which of them should be the gentleman in the next performance. This having been settled, the game was played through to the end, watched by the entranced Ted Pluto, who till then was more greatly interested in the play than in the prop which gleamed like the Pacific Ocean under the noonday sun.

With a mental shock he was forcibly reminded of the

blue glass dagger and all that Sergeant Crome had said about the missing haft.

"Let's have a look," he asked the little girl, hand outstretched.

Gazing into his round and smiling face, she permitted him to lift the 'jool' attached by the string to her neck, and one of the boys shouted that it was only a bit of old glass they had found. Ted examined it closely. There could be no mistake. The marks of the file and the smooth facet at the break were sharply clear.

"Give you a shillin' for it," he said.

The boys accepted the offer, but the girl declined. Ted raised the offer by a shilling, and the boys became excitedly eager to close. Still the little girl objected, not to the amount of the offer but to parting with the pretty 'jool'. The tracker persisted, raised the offer by yet another shilling, and one of the boys snatched the glass from the girl, broke the string, and presented it with one hand, the other held out for the money.

The little girl burst into a storm of tears, and Ted Pluto was instantly compassionate. He had to have the haft of the dagger wanted so badly by Sergeant Crome, chiefly for the glory which would be his and lastly for the desirable pound of tobacco. Having gained possession of the haft, he was tempted to run away from the weeping girl and the shouting boys, and refrained from so doing only by his inherited sense of fair play.

"Who owns this bit of glass?" he asked above the uproar.

"I found it," one of the boys shouted.

"We all did," yelled the remaining three, and the girl stopped crying to add her claim. Ted remembered the waiting Chic Chic; was dismayed by the time he had dallied here.

"I'll give you all a shilling and be done with it. Yes or no?"

That settled it. And with the dagger haft rammed into his hip pocket, Ted Pluto hurried off to the Manse, his mind busy with excuses.

Arrived at the kitchen door, he was confronted by an indignant Chic Chic. She was a modern miss, and no aboriginal man was ever going to keep her waiting, or behave like the lord of the bushland. In up-to-date parlance she told Ted just where he got off, then cooled down and ran a critical eye over him before they set out for Sunday school.

The bulge of his hip pocket gave her another handle to turn.

"What you got there, Ted Pluto?" she demanded, pointing to his nether region. "You bin wasting money on another pipe, I s'pose."

A guilty hand flashed astern to feel the protuberance.

"Summit I got for the sergeant," replied Ted, withdrawing the glass haft.

"Ooh! Nice!" Chic Chic thrust forward a hand. Ted made no effort to place the 'jool' in that shapely hand of dark brown velvet, and Chic Chic stamped her well-shod foot. "Let me see that, Ted Pluto."

"Can't. Belongs to the police. 'Tisn't mine, Chic Chic."

The girl grabbed the hand and began a struggle to force it to give up its treasure. Ted Pluto came within an ace of cuffing her, and it was surprising that countless generations of lordly men failed to hold this young man to their iron influences, so that instead of cuffing her he placed his other hand over Chic Chic's hands fighting to obtain the lump of blue glass, and with wrist strength forced her hands away.

Nothing would have given him greater delight than to make Chic Chic a gift of this object. He was of a race of men who had never owned anything excepting freedom when they became old. Nothing belonged to the individual: everything to the tribe. Possessiveness had ever been non-existent, and if Chic Chic wanted the bit of glass, or his shirt, he would normally have given it to her, and she in turn would give it to another aborigine if he or she wanted it—for to have was not to possess.

But behind and in front was Sergeant Crome. And Sergeant Crome was a white man and, more, a white policeman. Sergeant Crome wanted that silly-looking lump of blue glass, and Sergeant Crome must have it.

Chic Chic began to cry. She couldn't understand Ted Pluto's going on like this. They were tears of disillusionment. Poor Ted attempted to comfort her, tried to explain that he must give up the thing to Sergeant Crome, that he and the other boys had been searching for it ever since the white woman had been killed, that Sergeant Crome had shouted and sworn it must be found. Chic Chic remained indifferent to Sergeant Crome. She loved Ted Pluto, and Ted Pluto refused her a bit of old glass.

"Go 'way! Go on, Ted Pluto, go 'way!" she screamed. "I don't want you here. I don't want you to take me to Sunday school. I'll tell Mrs. Playfair on you, and she'll tell the minister, and he'll soon tell you to get to hell out of it for keeps."

A white suitor would have surrendered, but despite the black man's partial assimilation by white civilisation, he remains his own man. He sees more to be drawn from the future than the present. When Chic Chic pushed him from the kitchen and slammed the door in his face, Ted Pluto turned away and sadly walked back to Headquarters.

From the piece of glass in his great hands Crome looked into the smilingly triumphant eyes of Ted Pluto and said:

"Good on you, Ted, my lad. Where did you find it?"

"I didn't find it, Sergeant," Ted replied. "I got it from a white girl playing in a street. She was with some white boys—playing hold-ups. I had to pay 'em five shillin' for it. You givit back five shillin', eh, Sergeant? And pound of tobacco, eh?"

"You never asked the kids where they found it?" persisted Crome without ire, almost nonchalantly, for to shout or bully would have been useless.

"No, Sergeant."

"Think we can find those kids? You remember the street?"

"Too right, Sergeant. I paid those kids five shillin'."

"Here's your five shillings, Ted. Come on. Let's find those kids."

Chic Chic was an unpleasant dream. The clouds shadowing the spirit of Ted Pluto vanished. He had done right, had behaved like a man, and Sergeant Crome was pleased with him, so much so that he invited Ted to get into the front seat of the car instead of the back. It was a fine afternoon, much better than going to that old Sunday school, even with Chic Chic. The sergeant didn't even object when Ted rolled a cigarette.

"Out towards the Manse, eh, Ted?" Crome asked.

"Yes, Sergeant." Half a mile of pleasant driving, and then Ted instructed the sergeant to follow a road cutting off an angle. It was good, giving orders like this, and there was no need to ration his tobacco, either, with that pound lot coming to him.

Ted told Crome to stop at the corner where the hold-up had been staged. There were now no children playing a game, and Sergeant Crome frowned and brought back the clouds to shadow the aboriginal spirit.

"Should have found out where those kids got the haft," he said severely. "Where's your brains, Ted? Never be a policeman going on like that. Now we've to find those kids, and there's a lot of 'em in Broken Hill. You'd know 'em again?"

"Course, Sergeant, I know 'em." Ted brightened. "P'raps they're spending the dough in the nearest lolly shop. In that next street there's a lolly shop."

"Good on you, Ted. You'll make a policeman after all."

The sun shone brightly on Ted Pluto, and his chest could be seen, almost, expanding with pride. On the kerb of the pavement outside the lolly shop sat two of the boys.

Crome stopped the car beside them, leaned out, and grinned.

"Good day!" he cried. "How's things?"

"Good dayee, mister!"

"Come here," Crome invited, and they stood on the running-board and leaned over the door to stare at the silver lying on a huge palm. "Remember that bit of glass you sold for five bob?"

"Yes, mister. We picked it up coupla days ago. True, mister."

"Think you could point out where you found it?"

"Too right, we could. Some way from here, though. You take us in the car an' we'll show you."

"Inside a garden it was, mister," added the second boy.

"All right! You go to the shop and buy four ices, and we'll take you along."

One of the boys accepted the coin and dashed into the shop, returning with four ice-cream cones. The sergeant handed them out. The boys climbed into the rear seat. Ted Pluto lived in heaven, and Crome drove with one hand whilst licking an ice.

Eventually he was directed to a street of substantial houses and pulled the car into the shadow cast by one of a number of pepper trees.

"In this street, you say?"

"Yes, mister. The garden's further down, though."

"Well, one of you boys stay here with Ted. The other can come and show me the place."

Crome got out and terminated the argument over which of the boys was to go with him. They strolled along the pavement under the pepper trees, passing garden gates, and under wide-spaced light standards.

"That's the gate, mister," the boy said, pointing ahead, and Crome told him not to shout and not to stop walking when they came to the gate.

They came to a double gateway, and one of the gates was open and appeared never to be shut. The grounds contained several ti-tree shrubs and a fine old pine, and the driveway curved to avoid the pine tree. Farther on in the same fence was a small wicket gate, with the ground about proving it was never used. The boy said:

"It was just inside that little gate, mister. Rod seen it first, though. He fetched me to see it, and I went in and got it."

Man and boy passed on to skirt more garden fences, and presently they turned about, and so again came to the little gate. Crome said nothing. He and the boy continued walking. Beyond the solitary pine tree stood a stone house, weathered and commodious, and of two storeys. He had seen it before.

There are very few stone-built, two-storeyed houses away from Argent Street.

CHAPTER TWENTY-ONE

The Fearful Burglar

Jimmy's world was so unstable that he was mentally giddy. Having to work by day and sleep by night was a prospect irksome and degrading. Evil influences were at work, and he felt unable to cope with them unless and until he could stage a rebellion and regain his freedom.

The worst menace was this damned Bonaparte, who seemed determined to cruel his pitch—giving orders and blackmailing him. Burgle a house for a handbag or a baby's dummy, or else! Take your pick! Just plain blackmail. Then there was the Attraction. She demanded that he prove his intentions by taking a steady job at the mines before she'd marry him. Give up independence to become a slave. Yes, Mr. White! No, Mr. Black! Watching the clock every morning, and again every afternoon. What a fate!

Being intelligent, Jimmy Nimmo knew that when a burglar falls in love the end of his career is in sight. And he was wise enough to know that to retire from the game when on top was to invite stagnation. What to do, therefore, when an Attraction just couldn't take it when you told her you were a respectable burglar? Not tell her, of course—and then you couldn't be a married respectable burglar. Blast! Why did he have to fall in love with a woman who wouldn't be a burglar's wife?

He must do something about this inactivity. To be an artistic screwsman you have to practise constantly, just as a concert artist must practise, and why not now?

Even as a lover Jimmy had no time for the moon. It interrupted business, was uncontrollable, an ally for the cops. Next week it would rule the night. He reached the two-storeyed house at midnight.

There she was, the House of his Dreams, large, spacious, solid. Standing at the little wicket gate, Jimmy could barely see the outline of the slate roof against the sky to one side of the solitary pine tree. His ground-work had been completed: habits of the occupants, type of locks and window fasteners. He could go in with no more trouble than entering Goldspink's shop.

He needn't take anything—much. Just go in for practice, to feel the thrill of deep stillness, to feel again that power of movement in a small world asleep. Before he decided, his feet had taken him into the garden via the wicket gate.

First to merge himself with the ti-tree bush. The wind sighed among the branches of the pine, and the sighing became a softly played tune when he stood beneath the tree with his back to its trunk. But a few yards distant was the front of the house. There were two windows either side of the spacious porch, and five windows to the upper floor. The front was in darkness.

To the right of the house stood a wooden garage containing no car and used chiefly for firewood. Between house and garage a wide path led to the rear entrance and the kitchen. The old dame must be at the back, as it wasn't yet a quarter after midnight, but he would have to make sure.

There was no light in the kitchen or other rear room, and Jimmy went back to the pine tree, perplexed and alert.

Two women lived here, and the rhythm of their lives did not appear to vary greatly. They used a room next the kitchen as a dining-room, but one occupied the top-floor front and the other the ground floor. About ten every evening one or other would go to the kitchen and prepare supper, which would be eaten in the dining-room, and then the younger woman would return to her part of the house and put out her light round about eleven, and the other would go to her upstairs room and keep her lights on until two.

Since the younger woman had been killed with a glass dagger, the other had continued the routine. To-night, almost two hours before the routine time, the upstairs lights were out.

Bad. You had to know where every occupant of a house was before you went in. It had been Jimmy's intention to prospect the ground-floor rooms, and now he could not be sure if Mrs. Dalton was asleep or on vacation. Either asleep or awake on the top floor, Mrs. Dalton would have been no worry, but not to know her exact location was to make an entry unethical.

Peculiar, how it had all turned out. Before the female cop had been done in, Jimmy the Screwsman had stood under this tree on a dozen or more nights and had wandered round to the back to see the women in the kitchen or dining-room. They appeared to get along very well, but they certainly occupied separate quarters, as though each had her own flat. Occasionally they had gone out together, but were never later than midnight in returning home. They had had no visitors, and nobody remotely like Tuttaway had called—not when Jimmy had been around.

On two of his visits Mrs. Dalton had been sick and he had watched the younger woman leave the kitchen with a dish piled high with diced raw meat. On those occasions the lights on both floors had burned all night.

It seemed obvious that the female cop had said nothing about meeting with Tuttaway. Not so much of the female about her either. Supposed to be a man hater. Since when! Walking at night with a man, and such a bloke as G. H. Tuttaway.

Time slipped. Jimmy's watch, luminous only when he raised it to within an inch or so of his eyes, said it was twenty-four past one. He was suddenly conscious that his legs ached from standing so long against the tree trunk, and then he was aware of movement having nothing to do with the pine tree.

It was between the garage and the house, coming towards him along the house wall like a black beetle on a black curtain. Must have come in through the back gate off the rear lane. Not a bad route to come by, although the laneway was littered with garbage cans.

The man passed round the house corner and stopped at the first window. Jimmy could not make out what he was up to. Or when he passed on to the second window and stopped there.

Movement at the sill of the upstairs window above the porch. It looked like a bird perched up there, about the size of a crow or a magpie, but it didn't move like a bird.

The man left the window and went up the two wide steps to the porch door, and Jimmy lost him. The object on the sill moved, became larger, resolved into the shape of a human head. It could only be Mrs. Dalton, and she was leaning well forward, trying to see the man at the front door, and frustrated by the narrow porch roof.

A cop testing doors and windows! Very unlikely, here in Broken Hill, and beyond Argent Street. Another professional! Could be. The windows were easy. The front door was out. Besides a Yale lock, there was an inside door-chain.

The man left the porch, and the head above the upper sill became small and then still as the woman drew back a little. The man went on to the next window, remained there, went on again to the next. It seemed to Jimmy he stayed by that window for a long time, and he was beginning to wonder why, when he decided the man was standing with his back to the window and waiting for something to happen or some-one to join him.

Well, you can be lucky. If Jimmy had gone in he might have been bailed up in a flood of light and per-suaded by a pistol to remain whilst Mrs. Dalton tele-phoned the cops. And he could have done little about it.

Must be a cop standing there with his back to the window. No real pro would behave like that. No . . . Tuttaway! The chill of glass slid up Jimmy's back and remained between his shoulders. Tuttaway! He had bumped off one sister and was thinking of bumping off the other. And the other knew and was watching him, watching him from a dark window in a dark house.

The telephone! Why hadn't she telephoned the police? Perhaps she had, and the cops were even then on their way. No place for Jimmy Nimmo.

Wait! Think, you lovesick fool! The cops might already be on the job, already surrounding the grounds, moving inward to surround the house itself. The man at the window was waiting for the chance to get away.

He was taking it now. Coming directly to the pine tree, perhaps to hide among the branches, perhaps to trek to the nearest ti-tree bush. There was no sense in waiting for a man who might have another glass knife with the blade nicely filed ready to be snapped off when the deed was done.

Jimmy slid round the trunk and, keeping it between the man and himself, retreated to the nearest bush. Better to back into Sergeant Crome and do a stretch than meet a murderous maniac. From the bush he slid silently to the next one, breathlessly to reach the low fence.

No cops—as yet. But the man was certainly coming his way. Beyond the road and the low houses and trees on its far side, the sky was pale with the reflected arc lamps on the mines. He'd be a clear silhouette if he climbed the fence. Jimmy lay flat at the base of the fence and hoped he wouldn't be used as a step.

The unknown went out through the open front gate. Still no cops. Jimmy couldn't pause, and he couldn't hurry, for the man stood at the kerb of the pavement as though waiting for a tram or something. He could just be seen against the outer glow of the nearest street light.

Then he vanished and Jimmy waited to hear footsteps coming his way, gave him ten seconds, and slid over the low fence and walked rapidly in the other direction. Ahead of him was another street light, on the other side of the road, and it was the only one. Jimmy did not dally.

He had proceeded fifty yards, hugging the fences, keeping close to pepper trees, when he knew he was being followed. How? Not by sight. Not by sound. By the screwsman's Instinct out of Time by Experience.

He kept on, resisting the urge to run. On reaching the end of the street, he rounded the corner and vaulted a gate and crouched below the top rail. Here were no trees. The starlight was enough to reveal anyone coming round that corner. No one did. There wasn't a sound save the low rumble of the mine machinery. Instinct must have betrayed him.

Again he vaulted the gate and went on. He should have gone the other way, round that corner, made sure Tuttaway wasn't lurking there, waiting and watching. Always take Fear by the throat.

He *was* being followed. No mistake—no imagination about it. There was no sound, and nothing moved behind him, but he was being followed.

This street took him to a main road. It was a wide road, and light standards were on either side. It was almost 3 a.m. For the first time in his career Jimmy regretted he didn't carry a gun. He was still being trailed. No cop could walk as silently as this shadow. No cop could conceal himself like this lunatic.

Jimmy came to a small shop and slipped into the dark doorway to peer in the direction he had come. Still he saw nothing—and heard nothing save the distant roar of machinery on the broken hill.

This could not go on. Where were his nerves of steel? Might as well get married, if he'd slipped that badly. Farther along the street was yet another light, and he kept on, trying not to hurry, reached the circle of illumination, passed through it to the far darkness, and turned and waited. He saw the follower enter the light. He saw the fellow raise a hand signalling stop.

He should have known it.

What the bloody hell was the use?

He might have guessed it was that damned Bonaparte.

CHAPTER TWENTY-TWO

Why Extra Meat?

Jimmy was given the only chair in Bony's bedroom, and Bony sat on the bed and poured beer into tumblers.

"Surely, Jimmy, you are not interested professionally in that house?"

"I was. I'm not."

Jimmy drank without the usual reference to Luck. He was sour, and Bony countered the mood with gentleness. He waited for an explanation before saying thoughtfully:

"It's a good night for a burglary. Did you enter?"

"You know damn well I didn't."

"I seldom ask questions without reason, Jimmy."

"You weren't testing the windows and the front door? You didn't fox me to the fence and then follow me all the way to that street light?"

"I was not testing doors and windows, and I did not see you until you climbed over the fence. I was then approaching that front fence, and I stood against a pepper tree to permit you to pass. Guilty of following you from the tree. By the way, my pride is hurt. How did you know you were being trailed?"

Jimmy sighed, and Bony again filled his glass.

"You're no mug at trailin'," he said with assurance. "I never heard you, never saw you, not even a smell.

My scalp told me I was being dogged. I didn't like it, 'cos I was thinking things."

"What things?"

"A glass knife between me shoulders, and the haft being snapped."

"Let me have the story behind that thought."

Jimmy omitted nothing, proving ability as a raconteur, and when done, Bony brought another bottle from the wardrobe.

"You are sure it was a woman watching from the upstairs window?"

"Sure about everything. Why didn't she telephone the cops? She's got a phone."

"An interesting point, I agree. What gave you the impression that the man could be Tuttaway?"

"Look at the set-up," Jimmy almost pleaded. "It's gone one in the morning. It's a dark night. A bloke is walking round the joint and stopping to admire every window and the front door, and probably the back door. He could be a working pro, like me, prospecting the joint before timing the job. When he stood for some time in one place, I thought he must be a policeman until I recollected the dame who was watching him from up top.

"Then I argued that it wouldn't be a pro, for he wouldn't hang around after doin' his prospectin', and he had no reason to wait if he wanted to go in. It wouldn't be a policeman, not even you, waiting about like that. That's what I thought. I thought that the old girl must have phoned the cops, and close on that chunk of think I decided to scoot, but before I could get going the bloke came straight to the tree I was against.

"I couldn't be sure he hadn't screwed me off. The point what stuck in my mind was the old girl couldn't have phoned the police, and she was waiting in a dark house to watch that bird testing her windows and doors. She might have seen him prowling around before and expected him to have another go. She wasn't expectin' me 'cos my clients never get the chance."

"Did he look anything like Tuttaway?" pressed Bony.

"Not that I could swear to. He was taller than you and me, and so is Tuttaway. Still, Tuttaway has never been a you or a me, and this gent moved like a pro. You never saw him?"

"No. He must have left in the opposite direction a few seconds before I arrived. It was probably friend Tuttaway. The haft of the glass dagger was found inside the wicket gate. He'd been there before to-night. How long have you been keeping that house under observation?"

"Off and on for a couple of months."

The beer failed to lift the gloom from Jimmy's face, and almost savagely he seized the second bottle and removed the metal cap with his teeth. Bony probed further into the habits of Mrs. Dalton and her sister, and learned of their arrangement of separate apartments excepting for meals. He could not assess the value of the item that Muriel Lodding took a dish of diced raw meat upstairs when her sister was ill.

"Several things don't angle to my mind," Jimmy said. "What d'you reckon they'd want eight pounds of steak for every day?"

"Eight pounds of meat per day for two women?"

"Eight pounds of steak a day is what I said. Extra to

porter-house and chops and legs of lamb at week-ends. And since the sister's been murdered the order's no different."

"Dogs?"

"Seen none. Or cats."

"What of other foods—bread, milk—since you know so much?"

"Ordinary for two women. You goin' to do nothing about that sneaker? Could be Tuttaway after Mrs. Dalton."

"There's a man posted there. He accompanied me. However, it's unlikely that the prowler will return to-night."

Jimmy grimaced.

"Think I'll give up working in any state where you happen to be. There's another angle I don't get. The front and back is kept tidy enough, and flowers and things them women tried to grow in winter. At the back, though, there's a bit of ground about four times the size of this room, fenced with wire netting and a little gate in it. They don't grow nothing inside that fence. The sort of plot used for burying things, far as I can make out."

"Kitchen refuse," suggested Bony, and Jimmy negatived this.

"People don't bury refuse in calico bags. Besides, the Council cart empties the tins in the back lane three times a week."

Bony rolled a cigarette and said before lighting it:

"You know, Jimmy, you are entertaining."

"I can be, Inspector. A feller like me can be very entertainin'."

"The butcher's name?"

"McWay, Main Street South."

"And the milkman?" pressed Bony, making a note.

"People named Ludkin—out at Umberumaka. The baker is Perry Brothers, South, and, bringing in our old pals, the wood merchant is Frederick Albert Goddard. He delivered wood there two days ago."

"Your information appears remarkably detailed, Jimmy."

"I've been payin' a coupla school kids to give what I couldn't get in daylight."

"Indeed! I'd like to meet them. They might tell even more. Yes, we'll give them an ice-cream tea at Favalora's Café. Try to have them there at four to-morrow afternoon. Anything else?"

"You've got the entire brain-box. Can I go home to bed sometime?"

"Right now, Jimmy. See you to-morrow at four."

Bony let Jimmy out by the front door, slept for three hours, and was up at six. He prospected for the kitchen, found the yardman there, who, having lit the stoves, was drinking tea with a liberal dash of the dog that had bitten him the previous evening. It was much too soon for polite conversation, and, refreshed by tea and biscuits, Bony reached Headquarters at seven. Crome was in his office.

"Nothing doing," Crome said. "Saw nothing; heard nothing."

"Not even a light switched on?"

"Not a glimmer. I went in as far as the pine tree and sat there till first sign of break o' day. You nab that prowler who came over the fence?"

"No. He turned out to be a dear friend of mine. We

205

arrived a little too late. My friend had been watching a man testing the house windows and doors. We could assume it was Tuttaway paying another visit to Mrs. Dalton's house."

"I said so."

"It would seem so," Bony corrected. "Now you go off to bed. To-night might yield much. When will Abbot report?"

"At eight. Anything I can do?" Crome asked hopefully.

"Nothing—till after you have slept. You'll be out of your bed again to-night. Hit the pillow while you may."

Sergeant Crome departed in irritable mood. He was not liking several matters, among which was Bony's evasiveness. The kids had found the haft of the dagger, and a blooming black tracker happened by sheer luck on the kids. He had sat half the night against the tree, and a blinking screwsman had been there before him and reported to Bony a mouthful, of which Bony said next to nothing. Bonaparte was always in front. And now he was ordered to bed and Bonaparte would work out another move and be farther ahead than ever.

Senior Detective Abbot came on duty, to find Bony waiting for him.

"Come and help me dig into Staff Records," Bony invited. "The clerk in charge will not be here yet?"

"No, sir."

"I am interested in Muriel Lodding," Bony said when they stood before a card index.

Abbot extracted the requisite card. It gave the date Lodding had joined the staff, the date of one promotion, the date she had been discharged dead. Bony sought for additional particulars, and Abbot produced a loose-leaf ledger and turned up the sheet devoted to Police-woman Lodding.

Abbot was told to go, and Bony studied the details of Lodding's service. She had invariably taken her leave when due, and on a number of occasions she had worked on Sunday and had Monday off. There was no reference to sick leave until the previous year, and the dates under this heading Bony rapidly noted.

Again in his office, he set out in tabulated form the notes he had made, and at once found that coincidence could not be claimed for the juxtaposition of dates. He went into Crome's office and studied the calendar nailed to the wall, then asked Switch to inform him when Superintendent Pavier arrived.

Pavier was going through the morning mail when Bony walked in.

"Won't keep you long, Super," he said, and was invited to be seated. "Reference your late secretary. I find that these last few months she had been granted sick leave. Can you tell me if she appeared to be ill at those times?"

"Jittery nerves, I believe," replied Pavier, a question in his eyes. "Told me she was worried about headaches, and she thought they might be a kind of migraine."

"D'you know if she consulted a doctor?"

"I don't know about that, Bonaparte. In Records if she did. Or ought to be."

"There's no reference to a doctor in Records. I find, too, that on an average of about once in two months she worked on Sunday and took the day off the following Monday. Why?"

"She didn't ask to work on Sunday that she might

have the Monday," Pavier said. "It occasionally happens that there is an accumulation of reports for Sydney which must be got off, and Lodding always consented to work on a Sunday when I asked her. She was a smart woman, and I am only now beginning to appreciate how much I relied on her. What's on your mind about her sick leave?"

"Take a glance at these notes."

Bony placed them before the Superintendent.

1. Lodding on sick leave October 22 to 26. (*Goldspink murdered October 28.*)
2. Lodding on sick leave December 19 to 21. (*Parsons murdered December 23.*)
3. Lodding on sick leave February 16 to 23. (*Gromberg murdered February 25.*)

Pavier looked hard at Bony, the frown drawing vertical lines between his eyes. The fingers of his left hand tap-tapped on the desk, and for seconds he was silent.

"Very odd, Bonaparte," he said. "In each case, on the second day after Lodding returned from sick leave a man was poisoned."

"There is a period of two months between the first and second murders, and two months between the second and third murders," Bony pointed out. "It's why I asked you about the Sunday work. Probably no significance, as she worked on Sundays at your request. She could not have arranged the work to bring about your request, I suppose?"

Pavier was emphatic that Lodding had not done so, and Bony evaded his probing questions and returned to his own office.

CHAPTER TWENTY-THREE

Bony is Sacked

Bony sat in Favalora's Café waiting for Jimmy Nimmo and his scouts.

Slightly more than two months ago, at the same hour, old Alfred Parsons had come here for a cup of tea and sandwiches. Much of his life was behind him, but he was enjoying his retirement and treading on no one's feet. Here he had read his magazine, had finished his tea, rose to his feet to go, and was confronted by Death.

We must all die. As the Book says: "There is a time to die".

There was Hans Gromberg, set in his ways and habits, secure in life, and feeling good with his tummy full of beer, and he had risen to his feet to face Death. It had been likewise with old Samuel Goldspink, a kindly man to whom business was the chief interest. There is certainly a time to die, but when those three men were claimed by Death, it wasn't their time to die.

At the scene of the second and third poisoning a woman had been present who carried the same handbag on both occasions. Other women remembered her, two with clarity for features and dress, and one of these reported having seen a baby's dummy in the handbag. When the suggestion had been put forward that this person might be a man impersonating a woman, both Mrs. Lucas and Mrs. Wallace discounted it. Their observation and judgment could be relied on—and yet!

The first of the murders had been committed after Tuttaway had escaped. Tuttaway was insane. He had stabbed to death a woman reputed to be satisfied with her job and her home life. But Lodding and Tuttaway had known each other in England, and they were seen together in Broken Hill. A woman carrying the remembered handbag was seen to enter an hotel, and within minutes the hotel was searched for her in vain. Tuttaway, the magician, could have walked into the hotel as a woman and, within seconds, walked out as another woman. Tuttaway had killed with a knife, not with cyanide—that is, as Tuttaway.

The murder of Muriel Lodding had insinuated itself into the investigation of the three poisoning cases. It appeared, at first, to have no possible connection with the killing of the three elderly bachelors, and because of this Bony had not seen Muriel Lodding's home until the previous evening. Tuttaway, being a bachelor and a careless eater, was linked with the cyanide victims. Logically, therefore, he was a possible victim of and not the poisoner.

There was the remarkable juxtapositon of the murder dates with Lodding's sick-leave dates, and the finding of the haft of the glass dagger inside the gate of the house now occupied only by the woman's sister. That proved that Tuttaway had been there at least once before Jimmy Nimmo had seen him.

Mrs. Dalton had watched him. When normally she

did not retire until two in the morning, last night at
1 a.m. her lights were out and she was watching a man
testing the defences of her house. Why?

Mrs. Dalton! Having no known pets, Mrs. Dalton
ordered eight pounds of meat daily in addition to normal
requirements! No extra milk or bread.

Was there someone else living in that house? Was
Tuttaway being harboured by Mrs. Dalton? Absurd, on
the face of it. Were Jimmy wrong about his guess about
Tuttaway being the man testing the windows, Tuttaway
could be holed up there.

A search of the house might reveal much, but was
there sufficient evidence on which to base an application
for a search warrant? Both Pavier and Crome had called
on Mrs. Dalton, and she had received them with no hint
of subterfuge or evasion.

Jimmy Nimmo! Yes, Jimmy Nimmo! Jimmy was
coming towards him, followed by two boys on whose
faces was plainly writ anticipation. Jimmy was looking
without enthusiasm for the red-haired waitress, and he
need not have worried because Bony had previously
asked her not to recognise either Jimmy or himself in
the presence of the boys.

Jimmy introduced them to Mr. Knapp, down from
his station in Queensland, and Bony told them that New
South Wales was even better than Queensland, and that
the Australian Eleven was sure to belt hell out of the
Englishmen at the coming Test Matches. They swiftly
assessed him, his romantic background, and with the
casualness of their generation accepted his suggestion of
double ices. They addressed each other as Bluey and
Blackie.

Both lived in the same street as did Mrs. Dalton. They understood that their friend was very sorry for Mrs. Dalton and that he was anxious to know everything about her so that he could help her now that she lived all alone. Bony thought the boys were far more interested in the ices than in Mr. Nimmo's good intentions.

"What do you think of Mrs. Dalton?" he asked the red-headed boy.

"Aw, I reckon she's all right, mister," replied Bluey. "Better'n the other one, the one who was bumped off. She was a bit sour. Mrs. Dalton sometimes gets me or Blackie to do summat for her, and she gives us sixpence."

"Gave me a shilling once for going down to ole Clouter with a message," remarked Blackie.

"Anyone staying with Mrs. Dalton since her sister was killed?"

"Don't think," replied Bluey, licking his fingers.

"No one trying to get in ahead of Mr. Nimmo, I suppose?"

"Don't know. Don't think. Pass them cakes, Blackie, and don't hog. You seen anyone staying with Mrs. Dalton?"

"Nope! An' don't you hog the cakes, either."

"Haven't seen a tall gent taking an interest in the place?" interposed Jimmy.

The boys were too busy at the moment to reply. Bony opened the subject of dogs, describing some of those on his alleged station, and this subject brought the casual question if Mrs. Dalton kept dogs.

"Nope," answered Bluey. "Had one once, though. Black an' tan bitser."

"Yes," mumbled Blackie through the cake. "Died. She buried him in the garden."

"H'm! Pity. How long ago was that?" asked Bony.

" 'Fore Christmas. Musta et sun't."

Jimmy put in his oar.

"Ah, well, dogs take keeping these days. What they get through is pretty good."

"That bitser musta," Blackie managed to say. "Mrs. Dalton usta get eight pounds of steak for him, anyway. Still does. Tom told me. He delivers it. Now that's a bit rummy, mister. What she want it for now?"

"Puppies, perhaps," suggested Bony.

"Don't think. Don't hear any."

"Cats, then?"

"Nope. No cats, either. Never seen any. You, Bluey?"

"Nope. P'raps she makes meat pies."

"And gives them to poor neighbours," suggested Bony. "Does Mrs. Dalton have many visitors?"

"Nope," replied Blackie, and Bluey said:

"Seen one old geezer going in."

"I haven't."

"I have that," argued Bluey, button of a nose twitching with sudden belligerency. "Seen her going in through the back. Seen her coming out. Our back's in the same lane, that's how I seen her."

"Another ice?" asked Bony. Why ask? There was no stopping these boys. He waited for the ices to be brought before continuing the interrogation.

"What was the old woman like?"

"Like? Aw, bit older 'n Mrs. Dalton. Wears specs, at least once she did. The other one, Miss Lodding, didn't like her."

"Indeed! When was this?"

"Long time ago, might be since Christmas, the old geezer went in and Miss Lodding saw her in the garden."

"Then what happened?" prompted Jimmy.

"Beaut blue. I watched over the back fence. Couldn't hear nothing, though, but they went at it, and the old geezer dropped her specs and then she picked 'em up and follered Miss Lodding inside."

"Seen the old lady since Miss Lodding was killed?"

"Yeh, once."

"And who buried the dog in the garden?"

"Mrs. Dalton. Seen her take it into the little plot. Dead all right. Seen her digging the hole. Never had no more dogs after that."

"Fenced in with netting," offered Blackie, sighing with near repletion. "She's always digging in that little plot, ain't she, Bluey?"

"Now and then she does. Plantin' sum't, I think. Can't get near enough to see."

"Doesn't Mrs. Dalton employ a man for the garden work?" Bony asked, and was answered with vigorous headshakes. "You have never been right inside the garden?"

"Nope," replied Blackie. "Went in once and got bailed up by Miss Lodding. Told me to get out and keep out. Sour old cow. Mrs. Dalton's all right, but she won't let us in her garden, either. When she wants us to go a message, she comes to the fence."

"You don't think that the old geezer you spoke about really lives with Mrs. Dalton?" Bony persisted.

"Don't think. Might, though. Didn't clear out that time Miss Lodding told her off, anyway."

"You don't remember what colour her handbag was, I suppose?"

"Nope," replied Bluey, and Blackie added a headshake. They had downed half a dozen ices apiece and cleaned up the cakes, and, in the vernacular, 'had had it'. They followed Jimmy and Bony to the street with less sprightliness than on entering the café. Bony bade them good-bye, ordered Jimmy to dine with him that night at six-thirty, and walked slowly to Headquarters. He was in his office less than a minute, when Crome came in.

"Stillman's here," he stated levelly. "In with the Chief."

"Is that so?" Bony steadily regarded the sergeant. He glanced at his watch. "I want just twelve hours. Will you help me to them?"

Crome was cautious, although willing.

"As much as I can. That bloke gets under my skin. Just as we were getting places, he barges in."

"Don't worry about him, Crome. Concentrate. Give me twelve hours and we may send Stillman back to Sydney with a pebble in his shoe. I want both you and Abbot to have dinner with me this evening. Six-thirty at my hotel."

The big man frowned, then grinned.

"We'll be there, and thanks."

"Clear off now and take Abbot with you. Any of your men about, you send home or far away. Stillman can begin in the morning, but this night is mine. Game?"

"Too ruddy right, I am. Abbot will be too." Crome grinned again, and this time with anticipation.

Bony listened to the departing footsteps and smiled.

Without haste he gathered his notes and data and placed them in his brief-case. The file on Tuttaway also went in. With haste he went to the detectives' general office and retrieved the pictures from the wall, and these, too, he added to the contents of the brief-case. Then he rang Luke Pavier, catching him at the office of his paper.

"Are you busy this evening?" he asked.

"Couple of functions to cover. Could tell the boss to go to hell."

"Avoid the first and refrain from the second. I am throwing a party at the Western Mail. Six-thirty. You will remember that I promised to let you in at the death. Your own word, meaning finale."

"I'll be right on the dot," chortled Luke. "Want a hand?"

"With what?"

"Stillman. I could bash while you held him."

"I'll bash him my way. Expect you at dinner. Don't mention it at home."

"Okey-doke."

Bony rang Sloan, asked for a secluded table and the very special favour of occupying that table for perhaps an hour after dinner. Wally Sloan granted the favour and bestowed another. He would himself wait on Bony and his guests.

Bony replaced the instrument on the desk, not on its cradle—and waited. Ten minutes elapsed. The instrument spluttered, died, and he guessed that Pavier wished his attendance at his office. With his chair pushed back, he rested his feet on the cleared desk, and to one side a pile of cigarettes.

Stillman came in.

Of Detective Inspector Stillman someone had said he had the address of a film star, the voice of a radio ace, and the mind of a weasel.

"Ah! Afternoon, Bonaparte. The Super was wanting you on the mat."

Bony waved a hand towards a chair, but Stillman elected to sit on a corner of the desk. He produced a gold cigarette-case monogrammed in blue, lit a cigarette, and casually wafted smoke towards Bony.

"I heard of your arrival," Bony said softly.

"Had to come, you know. The Heads insisted. You are leaving us, I understand."

"I am remaining in Broken Hill for another week, perhaps a month. Interested in mines and might write a book about them."

"They have been written up so often, don't you think? Better return home. Your people are becoming annoyed. Anyway, my aboriginal friend, I am taking over, and you will be wise to return to Brisbane by plane to-morrow. The bush is your spiritual home, Bonaparte. Tracking white criminals in a city is evidently not your *métier*."

"The pronunciation of the French is defective, Stillman."

"I have never boasted of my education," Stillman lisped. "You are finished here, so get out. Unfortunate, of course. Can't have that fellow Tuttaway running about Broken Hill. Might murder someone else while you and Crome are practising for the movies. As I inferred, these city-bred birds fly too high for persons like you. I never did believe in the reputation you have so carefully built up. To fall down on that cyanide murder

217

right under your nose and in the very pub you are stay-ing at doesn't surprise me."

"The information we sought from London should assist you."

"Yes, perhaps. I brought it with me. Pavier says you have made slight progress regarding Tuttaway." Still-man slid off the desk. "Well, I must get down to it, Bonaparte. Don't let me keep you. The relevant files and case reports are about somewhere?"

"Doubtless, Stillman." Bony rose from the desk chair and took up attaché case and hat. "As you pointed out, I am finished here, so that files and reports are of no interest to me. You'll know where to find them. Having the information from London, however, you should not need them."

At the door Bony turned. Stillman was watching him. Bony smiled, and Stillman found nothing warming in it. Quietly Bony passed out and closed the door, leaving Stillman in an empty office, and proceeded to Pavier's room.

"It would appear, sir, that I am to go," Bony said stiffly.

"Thought you were out. Been trying to get you. You've seen Stillman, obviously."

"Yes."

Pavier stood, saying earnestly:

"I received no prior notification from Sydney. Still-man walked in and presented an instruction terminating your seconding, with an order to you to return at once to Brisbane. Personally, I'm liking it less than you. It hasn't been done correctly, but the excuse was that Still-man would arrive before air-mail delivery."

"Why Stillman? We have discussed Stillman, but why send here a man who failed before and wriggled his way back to Sydney?"

"Knowing the Chief of the C.I.B., sending Stillman might have been prompted by the wish that he fail again. Enough rope . . . Anyway, this termination of your association with us wasn't done by Sydney. Letter here from C.I.B. Chief explains that. Read it."

"Not now. You are only imagining you are talking to me. You tried to contact me and found I was out. You will see me to-morrow at nine, and then you will execute the Order of Boot. Clear, sir?"

"Something coming to the boil, eh?"

"When events delay, one must hasten them, Super. I must not fail, ever. I want only twelve hours."

Superintendent Pavier nodded slowly. Gazing at a point above and beyond Bony's head, he said:

"Glad I can't obey that instruction till Bonaparte reports."

He continued to gaze above Bony's head, and Bony turned and went out. Other than the duty constable in the public office, there was a plain-clothes man. Of him Stillman was demanding to know where the detective staff were. Bony sauntered by to the door, and he heard the detective say:

"Don't rightly know, sir. All out on duty, I suppose, sir."

CHAPTER TWENTY-FOUR

Bony's Party

It was an excellent meal despite the rush service occasioned by the determination of the Australian staff to be finished as quickly as possible after seven—or else.

Of Bony's guests, Jimmy the Screwsman floundered beyond his depth. Luke Pavier was entirely at ease. Sergeant Crome was slightly diffident, and Senior Detective Abbot a trifle awed. Alert for the welfare of his guests, Bony controlled the conversation, breaking down barriers and making them feel that all were his friends. Even Jimmy Nimmo eventually mellowed.

Wally Sloan cleared away and brought coffee and a bottle of his finest brandy. The 'sir' was tailed to every sentence. When he had gone, Bony said:

"It's as well Inspector Stillman is holding the official fort. He was, however, somewhat perturbed to find that all but one of the detective staff were out on duty."

"Ah!" breathed Crome. "Which man was there, d'you know?"

"Not his name. Tall, fair-haired young man."

"Simmons. Idiot. I told him to keep clear," growled the sergeant. "Told 'em all to get out and keep out and lock up everything before they went. I'll have something to say to Simmons."

"Stillman left holding the bridle without the horse?" commented Luke hopefully.

"He hasn't even the bridle," Bony said. "I brought it with me. Sloan has locked it in the hotel safe. However, we'll mount him to-morrow, or when you gentlemen of the Detective Office return to duty. To-night is ours."

Crome stared at his host through cigar smoke. Abbot appeared expectant. Luke saw a vision of the stiff-backed Crome and the efficient Abbot, with Bony and himself and this strange Nimmo fellow, making merry and 'burning up' Argent Street. And then he remembered that this dinner was the prelude to serious stuff and concentrated on Bony.

"You will recall, Crome, that we asked Sydney to obtain certain information from London," Bony said. "That information Stillman has with him. Declined to pass it on."

"What the swine would do," Abbot said without ire.

"I'm reasonably sure that the information, if added to my knowledge, would enable us to finalise these murders within a few hours," Bony proceeded. "I am left to guess what that information is, and I intend to gamble on guessing correctly. Without knowing what I know, the London information will not give Stillman anything like a clear picture.

"I have information for you, and a proposal to make. Stillman brought from Sydney an instruction addressed to Superintendent Pavier, who is to inform me to-morrow that my service with the New South Wales Police Department is terminated. At nine to-morrow I shall have no authority in New South Wales. Stillman will be in full charge, and I do want that Stillman find himself in charge of exactly nothing.

"You, Crome and Abbot, know that these recent murders were extremely difficult to probe. Each murder scene was instantly cluttered by the crowding feet of men and women. There could be deducted not one reasonable motive, so that it was not possible to determine whether the murders were premeditated or committed on impulse.

"With the murder of Lodding, however, we came on the Great Scarsby, and almost in spite of our efforts on the cyanide cases they have become linked with the killing of Muriel Lodding. The strength of the link, I cannot even now assess.

"I cannot find a reasonable answer as to why those three men were selected murder victims. Insane hatred of elderly bachelors could not have been the reason for their selection by the murderer, because Patrick O'Hara, who barely escaped being poisoned, had twice been married.

"Those four men yet had one thing in common. Each one of them was a careless eater. It was the one thing which united them in the mind of the poisoner. Consider the state of mind wherein is born the fury to murder a man for a habit which creates in the sane mind merely a feeling of disgust. Then consider Tuttaway.

"Sixteen years ago, Muriel Lodding did secretarial work for Tuttaway, and after Tuttaway went on tour to the United States, Muriel Lodding and her sister, Mrs. Dalton, came to Australia. They were living here in Broken Hill when Tuttaway was indicted and put away during the Governor's pleasure. Then Tuttaway escaped and came to Broken Hill, the obvious reason being to murder the woman who had worked for him in England.

"Mrs. Dalton at first said there was no man in Lodding's life. Then she said that her sister had worked for Tuttaway. Tuttaway never came to the house. She knew next to nothing about Tuttaway. She and her sister had not discussed at length Tuttaway's career. And yet she did not hesitate to tell me that Tuttaway went on tour in the precise year we knew he did. That, I believe, was a slip.

"The handle of the glass knife which slew Muriel Lodding was found inside Mrs. Dalton's gate. For some considerable time the butcher has been delivering daily eight pounds of steak to Mrs. Dalton. There are no pets to account for the meat. Mrs. Dalton and her sister did not entertain, and we know that an elderly woman who wore glasses and a younger woman were seen to enter the house or leave it. An elderly woman is thought to have poisoned Goldspink and a younger woman to have poisoned Gromberg.

"Then we know that firewood has been delivered to Mrs. Dalton by a man named Goddard and, further, that in Goddard's wood-yard office are several tins of cyanide. We know that Mrs. Dalton's dog died suddenly. We know that a man went round her house testing doors and windows in the early hours and that Mrs. Dalton watched him from an upstairs window. Although there is a telephone, she did not communicate with the police."

Bony ceased speaking, and rolled another cigarette. Luke Pavier said:

"A madman's riddle."

"The answer must be in Mrs. Dalton's house, but there isn't sufficient evidence to ask for a search warrant. In any case, it is now too late for me to apply for one, and I can assure you that Stillman hasn't a fraction of what we have. Which brings me to what lies right under his supercilious nose."

Bony related the dates of Lodding's absences from duty owing to sickness, pointed out that the periods between the first and second and the second and third were approximately the same, and added the dates of the three poisonings.

"At first study we might assume that Lodding suffered severe headache, sought for and obtained leave of absence, and within forty hours after returning to duty went hunting a victim with cyanide," Bony continued. "But we know that Lodding was at work at Headquarters when those three men were killed, and we know that when O'Hara's life was attempted Muriel Lodding was dead. Question: 'When Lodding asked for sick leave, was it actually for herself?' Again, Mrs. Dalton's house may provide an answer.

"Now for my proposal. It will be dark in less than an hour, and if the evening sky was read aright it will be very dark. Almost immediately Jimmy and I will set out for Mrs. Dalton's house, and we will enter it to see what we can see and hear what we can hear. I would much like you, Crome and Abbot, to come with us as far as the garden, conceal yourselves, wait and watch, and be ready for a signal. And I would like you, Luke, to be with Crome to observe and take notes for your paper. I think it likely that the man watched by Mrs. Dalton last night will make an entry to-night. We shall permit

him to enter, to learn his purpose, to overpower him if
he should attack Mrs. Dalton. *And* I think that man is
Tuttaway.

"On consideration, if you think that you would rather
not be associated with this somewhat unethical procedure, I feel sure you will just forget about it and go
home to bed."

"Too early—for bed," Abbot pointed out.

"Not too early for me to get going, Mr. Beaut Friend,"
chirped the son of Superintendent Pavier.

Jimmy Nimmo was gripping the edge of the table. A
lunatic killer, an insane poisoner, and now a madman
detective. Was he coming in or going out? Abbot was
faintly smiling. Crome sat stolid, his grey eyes small and
sharp. It was he who broke down a wall of silence.

"I been in the department twenty-three years. This
job could be the finish of me."

"I've been in the department for eleven years, and I
don't care a damn if it is the finish of me," Abbot said.
"Could you tell us more, Inspector?"

Bony sipped brandy and drank the remainder of his
coffee, cold. Luke thought it should be the other way
about, but gave it up.

"Let us consider more of Tuttaway," Bony went on.
"After what was reported to you last night, or early this
morning, Crome, you are bound to place men on watch
for that window-testing man. Assuming he behaves to-
night as he did last night, and you arrest him and discover him to be Tuttaway, what have you on him?
Murder, you answer, and rightly, and Tuttaway is
returned to Victoria to gaol. What next? Will Tuttaway
oblige by telling why he attempted to enter the house?

It is doubtful. You have gained something, but far from what could be gained if Tuttaway did enter the house and if it was found that someone else in the house was responsible for poisoning three men. Are you going to apply for a search warrant, or are you going to ask Mrs. Dalton for permission to search her house? Why should she grant permission when you hold the murderer of her sister, the man who tried to break into her house to murder her?

"Let us assume that Jimmy and I enter the house and find nothing incriminating, nothing suggesting that anyone living there could have poisoned Goldspink and Company. We leave, and there is no harm done. We will assume that Jimmy and I are discovered by Mrs. Dalton, who raises blue hell and rings for the police. You need not be the police, but quietly return to your homes. Jimmy and I clear out—or take the knock. Having been pessimistic, let us be optimistic. We take Tuttaway, and we put on him or another responsibility for the death of those three men; we present the completed investigation to the Super in the morning—and Stillman can go back to Sydney on the first plane."

Again silence. Luke studied Jimmy Nimmo, with whose profession he was not acquainted, and wondered why Jimmy looked green under the pale yellow lights. He studied Abbot and Crome, and his lips lifted slightly in a sneer for men hesitating to accept such a splendid opportunity. Then Abbot said:

"I'll be with you, Inspector."

"You have my assurance that neither Jimmy nor I will pinch anything from the house," Bony aimed at Crome. "All I ask is that you won't pinch us."

The grimness about the sergeant's mouth faded. The lips twitched. He began to laugh softly, and the sound rose in pitch till it rumbled around the room. Pushing back his chair, he attempted to get to his feet, seemed frozen in the act.

"It's funnier than you'd read about," he declared. "I'll still be laughing if I'm chucked out of the department. Let's go."

"Sloan will be waiting to take us burglaring in his car," Bony said happily.

They rose together. Luke wanted to shake hands with everyone.

And Jimmy Nimmo was positively sure he wasn't as sane as he had been when he came to Broken Hill.

CHAPTER TWENTY-FIVE

Jimmy's Mecca

A full quarter mile from the two-storeyed house, Wally Sloan was asked to pull into the cavern beneath the branches of a pepper tree and put out the lights of the car. The nearest street lamp was a hundred-odd yards away.

"If you are investigated by a patrolling policeman, Sloan, you must invent your own explanation," Bony said. "It's barely half-past nine, and you may have to wait many hours."

"That'll be O.K. with me, sir. I'll wait till the band plays."

"Now, Jimmy, you and I will go to it. You others know what to do. Much depends on you. Be wary, although it's unlikely that Tuttaway will be in the garden before you, and don't interfere with him unless sure he is leaving the place."

Crome crossed his fingers and, with Abbot and Luke, prepared to wait thirty minutes. Jimmy and Bony slid out into the void, and the car door was silently closed. Three minutes later they entered the lane passing the rear of Mrs. Dalton's house.

"I'm not as familiar with the grounds as you are," Bony admitted. "But I have a general picture of the place. You take the left side of the house and I'll take the right, and we'll meet at the pine tree at the front. Clear?"

"Okey. What do we look for?"

"Anything unusual. First to survey. Second to plan. Third to operate."

"Who's the burglar, me or you?"

Bony chuckled and patted Jimmy's arm.

"If ever we go into partnership, Jimmy, there's no policeman living who would catch us."

Jimmy was first to arrive at the trysting tree, and there he stood with his back to the trunk as he had done the previous night. It was so dark the ground was invisible and the house without form. Two illumined windows on the upper floor were like golden plaques. Waiting for Bony, he watched for him and flinched when a hand gripped his arm. The voice was familiar, like a voice in the memory.

"My side of the house is in darkness. There's a tool shed and a kind of summerhouse. No one in them."

"There's a light in the kitchen on my side, and the blind's down," Jimmy reported. "I poked into the garage and made sure no one's twiddling his thumbs in there. While I been here a woman passed across the blind in the right top room. Where we go from here?"

"You know the windows."

"The window . . ."

Jimmy's voice trailed into the dull ringing of the telephone within the house. Crome had said the telephone was in the hall. Bony waited. The bell continued. Light appeared at the transom above the front door. The ringing bell stopped. Neither man spoke until the hall light went out. Jimmy waited a half minute before saying:

"The window next the kitchen is easy. There's another easy one on the other side of the house. That's the one for me."

"Which one round the corner?"

"Second."

"I'll make for it. Give me a minute before you follow —in case anyone should follow me."

Jimmy counted the seconds before leaving the tree and proceeded by moving each foot low to the ground to feel for any obstruction. The clouds had switched off the stars, and it was a night such as Jimmy loved. Now, however, he wanted just a little starlight that he might be warned of the proximity of the man who had broken one glass kife and could have another he'd like to break. The distant street light beyond the front fence and the metallic glow of the mines in the eastern sector of the invisible sky provided no consolation. He was glad to reach the house corner and hug the wall till he came to the yielding obstruction which was Bonaparte.

"What's in here?" breathed Bony.

"Lodding's bedroom."

"How d'you know?"

"Saw it before she pulled down the blind. More'n once, too. The room to the front is a lounge. Beyond that is the hall, and t'other side of the hall is another lounge—where Crome and Pavier quizzed the old girl, you'll remember."

"All set, Jimmy. We'll go in."

To Bony it appeared that the screwsman became part of the window. He heard no sound. Jimmy spoke:

"She's jake."

Bony felt the window. It was raised. Beyond he could feel a blind and lace curtains. He slid over the sill, stood within the room, waited. Jimmy entered. An alert dog might have heard them, but Bony doubted it.

Jimmy rearranged the disturbed blind, intending to leave the window open—a way of retreat—but Bony pointed out that because Tuttaway probably would examine all windows he must not discover that one open.

Jimmy had to admit admiration, and satisfaction, too, for and with his partner this night. Bony stood with him in the ink-black room, feeling the spirit of the place and what lay beyond it, sniffing the scents which can tell so much from so little.

The air was stale, to be felt rather than smelled. There were two distinct odours. Napthalene and the perfume of cosmetics, and there was something neither could determine, a musty smell of decay beaten back by the perfume and the napthalene. Silence, a slumbering silence, was undisturbed by the noise of the far-away mines, which could not penetrate these old stone walls and expertly fitted window. There was no light until a dull opaque disc marked Bony's heavily shrouded electric torch.

The layers of the handkerchief were reduced until the disc emitted a short diaphanous beam without form. The beam moved. An easy-chair crouched like a petrified troglodyte to one side of a massive steel fireplace, blackly gleaming. A small table bearing an electric lamp and two books swung into being, and then the bed beside which stood the table, a three-quarter-size bed, made ready, as though for the woman who would never return.

The dressing-table appointments were expensive and in excellent taste. The chest of drawers and the wardrobe were old-fashioned and of rosewood. The clothing within appeared to be beyond the reach of policewomen and the wives of police inspectors. There was nothing of value to Bony in this room save the pictures on the walls. There were five, and all were photographic enlargements of a woman in period costumes.

"Passage outside this room?" Bony asked Jimmy, who had accompanied him on the tour of inspection.

"Don't know. To the front is the lounge room the Lodding woman used. To the back two more rooms. Blinds are always down. Must be empty."

"We'll examine the lounge."

Jimmy's slim hand closed about the door handle, slowly turned it. The door was locked. Steel glinted in the other hand, and steel teeth entered the lock. The door was opened without sound. The passage waited, darkly.

Jimmy closed the door after them but did not re-lock it. Bony glided to the door of the lounge. It was locked. Again Jimmy turned a key and opened a door.

Their feet sank into thick pile. The torch revealed the gleaming outlines of polished wood and the pattern of upholstery, the shapes of small tables, a writing-desk. Glass protecting a large bookcase behaved like mirrors. Jimmy crossed to the windows to make sure they were thoroughly masked.

Yet another massive steel fireplace, the grate concealed by a low screen of floral design. Above the mantel stood the youthful Queen Victoria. She was like someone Bony knew but could not recall. The picture was in oils and unsigned. Against another wall stood either Empress Josephine or Madame de Pompadour, also in oils, and the face was like that of Queen Victoria, and yet different. The resemblance was in the eyes. Bony again looked upon Queen Victoria. It *was* the eyes. And at some time he had looked into those eyes. He was sure of it.

The eyes, he felt, watched him as he moved the torch beam along the books in the glass case, as he examined the writing-desk, as he explored the contents of the camphorwood chest set between the two windows.

Again he stood before Queen Victoria. There was something about her mouth too. Ah! The mouth resembled that of Mills's drawing of the woman seen by Mrs. Wallace. He leaned against the mantel, lowered the beam of his light, strove to remember, and the beam fell behind the fire screen to reveal the grate filled with coloured paper ribbons.

Among the coloured paper something gleamed like gold.

Bony removed the screen and the paper, disclosing a large tin. Jimmy held the torch, and when Bony lifted out the tin he saw it was fitted with a press-on lid. There was no label. The metal was quite clean.

"Open it, Jimmy."

Jimmy removed the lid with his window-opener. The torch beam revealed its contents to be dark in colour, part powder, part lumpy.

"Cocoa?" guessed Jimmy.

"No, cyanide. Put the lid on."

" 'Struth! 'Nough to kill an army."

The tin was put back among the paper and the fire screen replaced.

"We'll go through the other lounge on this floor," Bony said, and they passed into the passage which immediately gave entry to the hall.

Beyond the hall a second passage reflected light from the kitchen. It was sufficiently strong to reveal the carpet, the hat-stand, a Jacobean chest, a wall mirror, a small table bearing a bowl of artificial flowers, and the front and lounge doors.

Silently they crossed the hall, observing that where the staircase was flush with the wall it was blocked by a polished wood door. Four steps led to the door: noted by men who missed nothing. They stopped at the passage leading to the lighted kitchen. No sound came from the kitchen. No sound came from above. Bony estimated that from the hall to the kitchen was fifty feet, with one door to the right and two to the left.

Where was Mrs. Dalton?

"Stay here," he told Jimmy. "I'll take a chance to see what is in the kitchen."

Jimmy waited, seeing Bony steal along the passage to pause outside the kitchen door, edge round the frame, and enter.

The kitchen was roomy. The wood range was polished like ebony. The table was scrubbed white. The dresser was decorated with green-spotted china. The usual cupboard beside the range, filled with pots and pans. A tall cupboard contained brooms. The dresser was fitted with two drawers above a cupboard. One contained cutlery, table mats. The second drawer contained a meat saw, two butcher's knives, and a butcher's steel. The cupboard held two new buckets and six chaff bags. In another cupboard was a used bucket, floor polish, and mop heads.

The meat saw was brand new. The butcher's knives were new. The steel had never been used. They were set out as though displayed in the window of a hardware store.

There was a scullery off the kitchen, but Bony could delay no longer and drifted back to Jimmy.

Together they 'went through' the second lounge, furnished formally and without the intimate objects found in that other lounge once occupied by Muriel Lodding. Leaving this room, they re-crossed the hall and sat in the mouth of the passage leading to the bedrooms.

"Just as well be comfortable while we wait," Bony said. "Wish I could smoke. What do you think they would want with a butcher's meat saw and knives?"

"Well, a butcher wants 'em to cut up carcasses." Jimmy was silent for many seconds before gripping Bony's arm and asking:

"Where was those things?"

"In a drawer of the dresser, laid out as though ready for employment. Never been used yet. Clean—and sharp."

Silence again. Then Jimmy:

"Can't get that stink."

"I should know it."

Again silence—a long silence. A board creaked and both men were on their feet. Another board creaked. Someone was coming down the stairs. The hall light blinded them, and instinctively they withdrew farther into the passage.

They heard the stair door open, and then they beheld Queen Elizabeth stepping down the hall—as though from a throne to forgive again her Essex. The years had ravaged her face, but the royal dignity was superb. She turned to the kitchen passage. In each hand she held a white Persian cat. She held them by their back legs. They made no protest. They were dead.

She could have taken the cats no farther than the kitchen, for almost at once she returned and mounted the steps to the door, closed it. The lights went out. A board creaked. Then another.

"Ninth and thirteenth treads, remember," Bony murmured.

"Them cats dead—or me?" Jimmy asked.

Minutes passed—perhaps five—when again the first of two stair treads creaked.

"Hell! She's coming down again," Jimmy hissed.

The hall light flashed up. They heard the stair door open. They saw Marie Antoinette step down to the hall. She was magnificent. She carried in each hand a Persian cat, held them by the back legs. They were dead.

Marie Antoinette disappeared kitchenwards, reappeared without the cats, went upstairs. The hall was blacked out. Jimmy moaned.

"How many more?" he asked fiercely.

"Queens or cats?" countered Bony.

Prolonged silence, until Jimmy plaintively asked:

"What *is* this joint?" No answer from Bony. "I'll tell you, then. Lunatics' Retreat, that's what it is. Do we have to stay?"

Further silence, this time terminated by knuckles upon wood. There was someone at the front door.

CHAPTER TWENTY-SIX

Henry and Dear Henrietta

"Back to the bedroom," ordered Bony. "Have both window and door open for a fast getaway."

The man on the porch—it could not possibly be a woman—again thudded a fist against the door, insistently, rudely. The sound was swallowed by the house, without echo, and in the ensuing silence the creak of the stair treads seemed almost as loud as the knocking. The hall light flashed up, and the stair door was opened.

Descending to the hall came Mrs. Dalton. She walked slowly, and with something of the sleepwalker, to the front door. Deep within the passage Bony heard her release the chain and turn the key. On again seeing her, she was backing to the centre of the hall, and there said harshly:

"Come in."

The door was shut and the key turned. A clergyman appeared, a tall man and stooping, with white hair and ragged beard. The hands clasping the round clerical hat were large and capable.

"Forgive me for calling at so late an hour," he said mellifluously, as though the years of intoning Gregorian chants could not be put aside. The woman's voice was icy.

"So considerate of you to telephone. Having watched you last night, I expected you to enter by a window."

"It was my intention, but, madam, I decided it would be undignified and, ah, unoriginal, in vew of my errand. I am happy to find you looking so well."

"I cannot compliment you on your role. The hair——"

"Required only for street lights. Pardon me."

The beard vanished. The white hair became grey and short. The figure gained in stature, lost its frailty. A handkerchief appeared, to be used as though to wipe the face of perspiration. The mopping done, the face was that in the Tuttaway file. The man stood as though awaiting applause, and said when Mrs. Dalton was silent:

"Are you not going to invite me to your sitting-room? Perhaps a little refreshment? I am indeed your sorely tried brother."

"State your business and go."

"It demands time, dear Henrietta. One does not gulp good wine. Let us be comfortable, for there is much to discuss, to achieve the grand finale. Unless for the purpose of art, haste of movement and of speech is unseemly. Therefore—lead on."

The same mocking voice. The insolent bow. The old stagey artificiality. The woman's breast rose and fell as though she had held her breathing. Her expression was of resignation as with a slight shrug she turned to the stairs. Her back was to the visitor, her face cold, remote, triumphant.

She went on and up, and Tuttaway followed, leaving the stair door open. Mrs. Dalton told him to switch off the hall light and where to find the switch. Bony slipped into the darkened hall. He watched them mounting the stairs. Save for a room light, the upper floor was in darkness. Against this light, first one and then the other was sharply silhouetted. The carpeted landing muted their footsteps, and without sound they passed from Bony's view. Then he heard their voices in the lighted room but could not distinguish the words.

He went up the stairs, to stand on the landing and within the deep shadows. In the lighted room the two were seated either side of a low hexagonal table bearing a bronze Eros, a silver box of cigarettes, and ash-trays. Tuttaway occupied a straight-backed chair. His hands were interlocked and resting on his crossed legs.

Beyond Mrs. Dalton was a settee, and on the settee lay an Elizabethan ruff, the gown worn by Marie Antoinette, and a navy-blue handbag having red drawstrings. To Tuttaway's left was a fireplace, and on the hearth-rug lay five white cats.

"After all these years, dear Henrietta, I am so glad to see you," boomed the Great Scarsby. "So many gales have howled across the Atlantic since we parted; so much has passed into the silence of time."

"I am not glad to see you," Mrs. Dalton said tonelessly, and her following statement was made also without emotion. "I've disliked many men and hated but one. Such is my loathing and hatred of you that words to express it are not to be found in any language."

"Hatred is warmer than love, my sweet," Tuttaway chided. "Hate does endure. Believe me, I know. And waiting stokes the fires of hate. I know that too. I have waited so long.

"Since the moment I returned to the house in London

and found you and dear Muriel absent, I have never doubted we would meet again. I was naturally grieved to discover you had deserted me, but heartbroken that Muriel had gone with you. You knew so well my hopes for her, my ambitions. Your plan was laid bare in that awful moment. You feigned illness when we were to embark for America, and you planned that Muriel should run away from me and slink back to London."

The man appeared about to weep.

"All my affection for you, dear Henrietta, went for nothing, meant nothing to your callous heart. All my love for Muriel was scorned, mocked. That girl had great gifts, and despite her stubbornness I would have made her famous throughout the world. You were jealous. You stood between us. I took Muriel from the gutter to make her great, and you thought to hide her from me. How stupid! Of course you were always mad, and I should not have trusted you."

"It is you, Henry, who has always been mad."

"Poor Henrietta," he drawled, his eyes like small agates. "The mad invariably consider themselves sane and all others mad. It is proof of your madness. When a child you were mad. Remember when you were in pigtails and I found you by the brook quite naked and with half a hundred worms in your hair? Had I not loved you, trusted you, protected you, you would have been certified like poor Hetty."

"I am not insane, Henry. I was born with a gift of humour. It was always you who couldn't see a joke. See a joke! A calculating sadist is incapable of appreciating a joke. A sadist can only destroy and glory in destroying lovely things. You killed Muriel's affection for you and in its place put fear. She was grateful to you for bringing her from that filthy tenement, for having her educated, for giving her ambition and dreams—and you killed her gratitude because you couldn't possibly do else but kill it. She loved me, but you even killed that. And in the end you must kill her body."

"Dear, dear! How melodramatic we are! Surely you will not accuse your own dear brother of murdering your cats?"

"Knowing you were going to enter this house, and with that foul purpose, I killed them that you should not torture them."

"With what did you put them to sleep?"

"With a little something obtained from the wood merchant. An obliging man. There's none left, so you won't poison me."

The man chuckled sonorously. He smiled, and without apparently looking at what he did he took a cigarette from the box, balanced it at the edge of the table, tapped the free end, and it fluttered to his lips. A hand went to a waistcoat pocket and came away with an ignited match.

"Mad! Of course you're mad, Henry. You raved even at Muriel. Slapping her face when she was tired. Tying her to a chair when she defied you, and making her watch you put her kitten into the stove and turn on the current, and laughing when she shrieked. You've always been mad: breaking little puppies' legs to see them limp, tying cats together by the tails and putting them on a clothes line to watch them fight to death. You will not torture my cats."

"I intended, dear Henrietta, to kill you mercifully. I

will reconsider that. You knew, of course, it was I when the papers reported the glass dagger?"

"I knew you would come here, knew it the instant you escaped. Muriel wanted to go away, but stayed for my sake. I waited. For you!"

"A glass dagger!" Tuttaway chuckled. He plucked a crimson dagger from his hair and another of jade green from behind an ear. "Remember when I bought these in that singular curio shop in Milan? You wanted me to share them with you and Muriel, and I would not because they were so beautiful lying on white satin within the glass-domed case. But I did promise, remember, to share them one day. To give the blue one to Muriel and the green one to you. Muriel received hers."

Mrs. Dalton did not speak. She smiled.

"And presently you will receive yours."

"You wouldn't have the courage to plunge the red dagger into your own body, Henry. I know that."

"The red one! Ah, Henrietta, that is for the girl for whose sake I was martyred. She married and went to England, whither I go a few weeks hence." The daggers vanished, and Tuttaway stubbed his cigarette and took another from the box. He stretched his legs and glanced about the room, nodded with satisfaction at something Bony could not see.

"I wasn't so foolish as to bury all my treasures in one hole," he said. "Much money, a few valuable diamonds, and the daggers I left in a safe-deposit vault, and some of my wardrobe and useful make-up boxes were hidden in a safe and secret place. I wasn't then decided what to do about you and Muriel.

"A fellow sufferer from man's inhumanity was to be

released, and I arranged with him to purchase clothes for me—these same clothes—and hire a drive-yourself car and be at a certain place on a certain date. It was quite easy. The car was stopped twice before we reached the city, and on both occasions the police apologised to 'his reverence'. You see, they looked for a madman, and I'm not mad. I needed no silly false beard and wig: merely reddened my face and expanded my cheeks with paper wads and used an Irish accent. Do I see beer on the cabinet?"

"I'll get you a drink, Henry."

"Pray do not trouble, dear Henrietta."

The stilted manner in which these two talked, especially Tuttaway, verged on the ridiculous. Not for an instant did they cease to watch each other. After Tuttaway left his chair to cross to the cabinet, Mrs. Dalton watched his every movement, and, from her attitude, Bony knew Tuttaway watched her.

On returning to his chair, he carried a bottle of beer under an arm, a tumbler in one hand, a bottle-opener between his teeth, and the green dagger in his other hand. He sat down before unloading.

"And then what did you do, Henry?" the woman asked.

"Sought you, of course. Found you had left Sydney for Broken Hill. Had I not been taken up with training that fool of a girl, I would have found you before you left Sydney. I was forced, therefore, to be cautious on coming here. Could not permit Muriel or you to hear I was making inquiries concerning you.

"What a large number of cats you have, dear Henrietta. Cats everywhere. So decorative, too. Mad! There is no doubt of it. I should have had you certified when you burned all my waistcoats. What a thing to do!"

The woman's mouth writhed. Her voice was low, vibrant, passionate.

"Still the sloppy, slobbering, drooling beast. I would have burned your revolting body with the clothes had I known then what you did to Muriel—making her kiss the filthy tainted things when she taxed you with it. You broke her, didn't you, Henry? Made yourself the great fear in her heart and mind, so that even my affection couldn't help her. A hero to the rest of the company, you were a beastly, bloated swine to Muriel."

The chuckle Tuttaway gave tautened Bony and sent ice up and down Jimmy's back.

"You should have known I would catch up with her and you. I merely had to meet her one evening when she was walking home. By that time I knew her habits, where she lived, all about you. So we went walking in the gloaming, and I told her how sorry I was, how misunderstood. She forgave me, Henrietta. When I told her how you had always been queer, she—well, she believed it. I have not lost the art of being charming despite the infliction of man's injustice. Those lies you told her, Henrietta. She remembered them. Then she said we were going the wrong way. She was strong. She always was."

"And then you killed her?"

"Put her gently to sleep, my Henrietta. She felt nothing."

Not for a second did his gaze leave her. She was breathing fast, and appeared gripped by terror of approaching death to be seen in his eyes and about his mouth. Drawing the tumbler to him, he took up the bottle and worked the opener with the hand steadying the bottle on the table. The beer frothed from the uncapped bottle, sprayed the cigarettes in the box, drenched Eros with white foam. He managed to fill the glass; the left hand gripped the haft of the green dagger.

He drank, and beer splashed over the clerical vest.

"You loathsome pig, Henry. Stop it! For heaven's sake stop it!" Mrs. Dalton's voice rose to a shriek. "All my life—all my life I've had to look at that beastly habit."

Came a mere flash of what was due.

"Your pardon, Henrietta. Careless of me . . ."

Tuttaway set down the half-empty glass, reached into a coat-tail pocket for a handkerchief, looked down at his vest to wipe away the liquid, and tucked a corner of the handkerchief behind the clerical collar. As he poured more beer into the glass, he leered at her.

"Well, my dear sister, I shall have to leave you." Jadegreen glass whirled about his hand like green mist. "I cannot face the thought that you will surely be put away if I do not negative the danger. In those places, you know, they do things to you. I shall be swift and gentle, for you are my sister and we did have fun."

"You mustn't be a fool, Henry."

"Oh no! Indeed, no!"

"Surely you realise you are dead?"

"Am I, dear Henrietta?"

"Of course. You are only a ghost."

The ghost smiled broadly. The chuckle came from deep within the ghostly belly. The ghost rose to its feet. The woman rose, too, as though his eyes impelled.

Tuttaway laughed, snatched up the glass of beer, bowed to his sister. The dagger lay flat along the palm of his right hand.

Mrs. Dalton's face was ashen.

Bony motioned Jimmy to enter the room after him. The pair facing each other over the table might easily have seen them had not each been concentrating on keeping captive the eyes of the other.

"My aim shall be true. This ghostly hand will not fail." The man's voice deepened, became sonorous. "We are about to part, and I give you fond farewell. Here's to the lass who was always loony. Here's to the saint who murdered her cats between playing the role of this queen and that. Here's to the idiot, her long life done, the years behind her and all their fun. Here's——"

"Dear Henry! Have done and drink your toast. And please—please, dear Henry—don't drool on to your waistcoat or I *shall* go mad!"

Tuttaway roared with mirth. Bony watched the hand holding the dagger. Jimmy Nimmo stood just behind him. Mrs. Dalton saw neither. She saw only George Henry Tuttaway, and Tuttaway saw only her.

"Madam, your very good health," he shouted and drank. The hand bore the dagger aloft and back over the shoulder for the throw. Bony jumped, landing upon the table, then crashing full into the Great Scarsby. Mrs. Dalton screamed:

"Leave him be! Look at him! He won't believe he's dead!"

Tuttaway gasped horribly. He gained his feet. The dagger slid from his hand to the floor. His teeth were bared in a dreadful grin as his body arched backward and his legs gave way. Mrs. Dalton began to laugh—softly, gleefully, like a child.

When? How? The bottle had not previously been opened, for the contents had cascaded when inelegantly uncapped. Never once had the woman received the chance to pass her hand over bottle or glass. Tuttaway had watched her every movement, save that one second he had looked down upon his soiled vest. Bony had missed nothing, and yet . . .

Mrs. Dalton's laughter softened to a throaty purring. "Get up, Henry, and be killed again. Don't lie there like a numbskull. You must rise that I may kill you again. It's the only joy you have given me. So clever, Henry, were you not? Clever! The Great Scarsby! The Great Mass of Rubbish! The Great Simpleton! See, Henry? My little syringe fitted with the bulb from a baby's dummy to give it greater force. Look, Henry! Get up and look. I'll show you."

She dashed beer into the glass and filled the syringe, oblivious of Bony and Jimmy, who stood at her side.

"The syringe is filled with liquid cyanide, dear Henry, and held crosswise in the palm of the hand. Can you see it? No. The quickness of the hand deceives the eye; you taught me that. You won't arise? Well, then, take it lying on your dirty back."

Both men were watching the woman's right hand, and both thought they imagined the amber bullet which sped into the open mouth of the dead man.

CHAPTER TWENTY-SEVEN

Bony Reports

Superintendent Pavier entered his office at a quarter to nine, and before he could seat himself at his desk his secretary came in to say that Inspector Stillman wished to see him on a matter of urgency.

Pavier sat down and fingered the unopened morning's correspondence. His apparent rudeness was but to gain time.

"Er—oh! Yes, Miss Ball. Tell Inspector Stillman to come in.

"Yes, Stillman, what is it?" he asked distantly when Stillman stood before him.

"I took over from Bonaparte at approximately five-twenty yesterday afternoon," Stillman said woodenly, as though giving evidence. "I have been unable to locate either Sergeant Crome or Senior Detective Abbot. The staff is also missing. I have searched for the official file on George Henry Tuttaway without success. It is now almost nine o'clock, and the Detective Office is still utterly deserted. It seems an extraordinary state of affairs, sir."

"H'm!" Pavier dropped the letter he had opened whilst Stillman was speaking. "Am I to understand that you took over from Bonaparte yesterday afternoon?"

"That is so, sir," Stillman replied, made wary by the glint in the eyes watching him.

"I assume I am the officer in charge of this division, Stillman. I hope to hear that Bonaparte told you to go to the devil. It is for him to be informed by me of the contents of Sydney's instruction."

"I thought it was understood——"

Bony walked in.

"Morning, Super!"

"Morning, Bonaparte!" Pavier returned, and Stillman gracefully stepped back, to savour in full the 'sacking' of this upstart. "I understand that Stillman has already spoken to you of an instruction he conveyed from Sydney. Er—here it is."

"Don't bother, Super." Bony drew a chair to the desk and sat down with his back to the standing Stillman. "I'm leaving for Brisbane on the 11.20 a.m. plane, and I have to call on Mrs. Robinov to pave the way for a romantic friend of mine. Here is the report on work accomplished for your division, and I would like to make a verbal report in the presence of two of your officers who have been splendidly co-operative and have revealed marked initiative. Would you kindly call for Sergeant Crome and Detective Abbot?"

Superintendent Pavier used the telephone, and whilst speaking glanced at the superscription on the foolscap envelope. It was addressed to him and marked: "Short-hand Notes and Transcriptions." The handwriting was that of his son. Crome and Abbot came in. Pavier looked quizzingly at Bony, who invited them to be seated. Stillman remained standing. No one saw him.

"Well, Super, we have tied up those homicide cases."

Bony began briskly. "In the morgue we have the murderer of Muriel Lodding, and in the lock-up we have the murderer of Goldspink, Parsons, and Gromberg. My report covers the investigation conducted by us since my arrival, and you will, I believe, find it clear and journalistically concise. As I said a moment ago, I am happy to commend Sergeant Crome, who has been most co-operative and keenly helpful, and Senior Detective Abbot, who has shown equal zeal and marked intelligence.

"I will run over the essential points. You will find in the report several additional items concerning the Tuttaway family history. Tuttaway himself was doubtless insane all his life, but because he had an outlet in creative work of a sort he was regarded as merely eccentric. He became, as we know, world-famous as a magician.

"In those early years of mounting success Tuttaway was accompanied by his sister Henrietta. She was as great as Tuttaway, and both were undoubted artists in their chosen *métier*." The word was split in pronunciation for Stillman's benefit. "Henrietta Tuttaway's finest work on the stage was to present half a dozen famous queens in history, making the changes so swiftly as to give the audience the impression of a procession of queens. She was also an expert sleight-of-hand performer.

"Henrietta admits her brother made her stage success possible. As a young girl she revealed incipient insanity, but her brother seems to have steered her clear of serious trouble. Eventually they bought a house in Ealing, London, and to the household Tuttaway introduced the girl we know as Muriel Lodding. It was his intention to train her to take her place in one of his shows. However, Muriel Lodding was not enthusiastic, and Tuttaway, naturally cruel, tormented her. The case in Victoria was a repetition of history.

"Muriel Lodding received deep affection from Henrietta. It became Henrietta's mission to protect her as much as possible from her brother, but as the years went by her mental health deteriorated and gave Muriel Lodding much concern. On tour in America, therefore, when Henrietta was left in the house in Ealing, Muriel ran away from the company and returned to England, and within a few days both women were on a ship coming to Australia. After arrival they changed their names and gave out they were sisters.

"Eventually they heard that the Great Scarsby had returned to London, and subsequently that he had arrived in Sydney. They found sanctuary in Broken Hill, and here Henrietta, who claims she is the widow of a man named Dalton, appeared to recover in health.

"Muriel Lodding's great fear was George Henry Tuttaway, who had exercised sadistic dominance over her. When he escaped, she wanted Mrs. Dalton to move on with her, even return to England, and the fact that she merely had to apply to you, sir, for police protection to ensure safety from the man seems to have been countered by Mrs. Dalton's determination to remain in Broken Hill and herself deal with her brother. We found placed ready in a kitchen drawer a butcher's meat saw, butcher's knives, and several hessian bags, and we now know that these articles were purchased by Mrs. Dalton ten days after the escape.

"It cannot be proved whether Muriel Lodding suspected Mrs. Dalton of poisoning those three men. Mrs. Dalton states that Lodding was not implicated, but I think, in view of the fact that three men were poisoned within two days following each of three mental illnesses suffered by Mrs. Dalton, and which occasioned Lodding to ask for sick leave, that Lodding must have suspected. We do know that Lodding once met Mrs. Dalton returning home in the guise of a much older woman, and her failure to report her suspicions was probably due to a sense of deep obligation to Mrs. Dalton.

"The effect of the escape on Mrs. Dalton was, in Dr. Hoadly's opinion, the subsequent mental upsets. During these upsets she had to be controlled. Following the crisis, when Lodding felt she could return to work, Mrs. Dalton's mind entered a secondary phase when she was not so completely mad as to appear in public dressed as Queen Victoria, and sufficiently sane to avoid through disguise the consequences of her phobia.

"This phobia, or hatred of her brother, was the product of several characteristics in the man, the major one being a long habit of feeding like an untrained child. To the sane, a mere pebble, but to Mrs. Dalton a volcano which erupted when he escaped. His escape drove her to seek men like him, and by poisoning them she received temporary satisfaction in having destroyed that which she loathed.

"She used a small syringe and, following practice, was able to conceal the instrument in her hand and squirt the poison accurately for a distance of two to three feet. The first two victims were selected. Gromberg she met in the street and followed to the hotel lounge, and O'Hara she saw beside the fountain. Both Miss Isaacs and Goldspink knew Mrs. Dalton, but so perfectly did she disguise herself that neither Goldspink nor any of his assistants recognised her that afternoon she poisoned him. Parsons habitually visited the café. She went there often as Mrs. Dalton, and most likely was not as Mrs. Dalton when she poisoned Parsons. The afternoon she poisoned Gromberg she was looking for a victim, and because she sometimes shopped at Mrs. Goddard's grocery store, she had rubber pads inside her cheeks and her nostrils to make her something like that woman."

Bony related the story of the glass daggers; of the meeting of Tuttaway with his sister in Mrs. Dalton's house; of what had transpired.

"It's all in my report, Super. Dr. Hoadly's preliminary report is attached. His opinion is that Mrs. Dalton is decidedly certifiable. Goddard and his store of poisons and other questionable possessions I leave to be investigated. And where Tuttaway has been living must also be left with you.

"To conclude. Tuttaway, the poseur, the actor, had to purchase gloves in Broken Hill, where the wearing of gloves is as rare as a top hat. Abbot produced George Henry Tuttaway from the Records, working only on a description given by a man who had seen him buying the gloves. The haft of the dagger used to kill Lodding was discovered by Crome to have been found inside Mrs. Dalton's garden gate. And I recalled seeing Muriel Lodding seated at her desk and abstractedly toying with a pencil. The pencil appeared to slide in and out of her fingers of its own volition, and so quickly as to make it appear to flow like brown water. That gave me the first link between her and the Great Scarsby.

"These have been cases requiring not only intelligence but patience. It demanded, too, the approach to witnesses as collaborators and not criminals. We met with many illogicalities, due to the mental state of both murderers, and they are so obvious as to be ignored in this, my verbal report. That, sir, finalises my investigation. My report has been ably drawn up by Mr. Luke Pavier, who, I am sure, will render through his newspaper honour to whom such is due."

Bony stood smiling at Superintendent Pavier. Pavier left his chair. Perhaps he guessed how the report was worded, for he said with unwonted warmth:

"Gentlemen, my congratulations. To you, Bonaparte, our thanks."

Bony shook hands with Crome and Abbot. With Pavier, they accompanied him to the door, and when shaking hands with the Superintendent, Bony said:

"*Au revoir!* I shall be returning in the near future. You see, I expect to be best man at a burglar's wedding."